THE BEND IN THE RIVER

He led her away from the crowd and the fireworks along a dark walk between thick belts of shrubs. When he stopped and took her in his arms, she yielded to his rough urgency, wanting to comfort him, help him forget the tormenting mind and the memories, and finally catching some of that urgency in her own response. She had frustrations and memories to blot out, too. When at last he released her, she was trembling. She leaned against him for a few moments, saying nothing, feeling the wild beating of her heart, while he moved his hand gently over her hair.

'I'm sorry, Tonie. I shouldn't have taken you with me this evening. A bad mood. I was using you. I . . .'

'No need to explain. I know. I was willing to be used. I wanted to help you.'

'Not used. I needed you.'

'A little, yes. We said console each other. Remember?'

'Sounds very neat, but you, my dear, are not a girl to do anything by halves, I fancy.'

The Bend in the River

Iris Bromige

CORONET BOOKS
Hodder and Stoughton

Copyright © 1975 by Iris Bromige

First published in Great Britain 1975 by
Hodder and Stoughton Limited

Coronet Edition 1976

Printed and bound in Great Britain for
Coronet Books, Hodder and Stoughton London
by Richard Clay (The Chaucer Press) Ltd
Bungay, Suffolk

ISBN 0 340 21000 1

Contents

*Love consists in this, that two solitudes
protect and touch and greet each other.*

RAINER MARIA RILKE

I

Remembrance of Things Past

MIRABEL RAINWOOD, SITTING at her bureau in the drawing-room, looked up from the diary in which she had been writing and gazed out of the window. It was a bright May day, with fleecy white clouds sailing across a blue sky. The garden was gay with wallflowers and pansies and tulips. And the old pear tree was in bloom. A fresh and dazzling month, May, full of colour and promise. She was glad to have been spared to see it come round again. At eighty-two, one treasured it all the more. She watched a chaffinch hopping among the white blossom of the hawthorn tree near the window, looking for insects. In a few moments, the bird flew off with a beak full of food for its young. What a pleasant shopping precinct, a may tree in bloom, she thought with a whimsicality rare in her, and turned back to her diary.

A letter from Pierre Valais this morning with the sad news of his grandfather's death. He is coming to see me on Friday with a package Louis left for me. And so today has been full of memories for me. Dear Louis. Those happy holidays in France, so long ago, and yet so vivid to me today, as though they happened only yesterday.

She stopped writing and gazed out of the window again,

seeing this time not a sunny English garden but the country lanes of Normandy, and a teenage girl with black plaits cycling along beside a dark-skinned boy with dancing black eyes and a voluble tongue. How they had argued, she and Louis, putting the world to rights. Picnics, bathing parties, tennis. And at seventeen, she had thought she might be falling in love with him, while Louis, two years her senior, had had no doubt. Letters had been exchanged during the intervals between those longed-for holidays until, soon after her eighteenth birthday, she had met Charles Rainwood and discovered the difference between an affectionate friendship and love.

She had married Charles the following year, distressed at the pain so evident in the at first reproachful and then unhappy letters she received from Louis. He had married some years later, and they had all met as friends whenever Mirabel visited her French grandparents, but always she seemed to see reproach in Louis' eyes. But the link between them had never been severed, for Louis' son, André, had escaped from occupied France to England during the war and had served in the Free French Army. During his training in England, he had kept in touch with Mirabel, had married an English girl, and after the war had settled in England. She guessed that it was at his father's prompting that André had asked Mirabel to be godmother to his second son, Pierre, thus strengthening the link.

Her thoughts returned from the past as her husband came in, pushing a tea-trolley.

"Thought it was time," he said, moving stiffly towards the window, pushing the trolley with the slow care enforced on him since the slight stroke suffered a year ago, which had affected one shoulder and leg. In spite of these disabilities, he insisted on drawing up a chair for his wife, glancing at her sharply as she sat down and took up the teapot.

"You look tired, Mirrie. Upset about Valais, no doubt. But at eighty-four ... a fair innings."

"Yes, of course. But it's always a shock. Part of one's life chopped off. A kind end, though, Pierre said. A short illness. I shall be glad to see Pierre again. He's very like his grandfather."

Charles said nothing, turning his attention to a buttered scone. That fellow, Louis Valais. Always sweet on Mirrie. Dashing chap. Handsome. A wonder Mirrie preferred me, he thought, for Charles Rainwood was essentially a modest man. He remembered the first time he had met Valais, when Mirrie had taken him to visit her French grandparents a few weeks after their engagement. The Valais family had come to dinner one evening while they were there. The furious hostility in Louis' eyes had hit him like a dagger beneath the almost exaggerated politeness. He sighed. A devilish long time ago. They had lived through two world wars since then. Had lived too long, maybe, into a world they neither liked nor understood. Or, at least, that was how he felt. Best not let Mirrie hear him express such sentiments, though. She had somehow managed to retain her confidence in life. She would merely tell him crisply that it was personal relationships that mattered in life, and that he looked at too many news programmes on television.

They sat there in companionable silence until Mirabel said reflectively, "It's three years since Pierre's wife died. I've only seen him once in all that time. I hope the poor boy has managed to put the pieces together again."

"Hardly a boy, Mirrie. What is he? Thirty or so?"

"Thirty last month," said Mirabel, who never forgot the birthdays of children, grandchildren, great-grandchildren, or god-children, numerous though they were.

"Didn't you tell me he'd left London after his wife died? Went abroad?"

"Yes. At least, that was his intention, I believe, but I've seen and heard so little from him of recent years. Claire's death completely shattered him, I heard, but on the one occasion when I saw him after that, he revealed nothing of his feelings and little of his plans. He wore a mask which I did not try to penetrate. Bereavement of that kind can only be helped by time. I'm hoping that the mask may no longer be needed, though, and that I shall see the old Pierre on Friday."

When Pierre Valais arrived on that Friday afternoon, however, Mirabel realised that a lot of the old Pierre had died with his wife, and that the present Pierre was a man not easily read. But the same quick, easy charm of his grandfather was there as he took her hands with a warm smile and said, "*Marraine*. As regal as ever," before kissing one of those hands in true Gallic style.

The weather, in the true tradition of English springs, had changed, and the day was cold and dull, making the fire on the hearth welcome. Mirabel sat in the hard high-backed chair which she favoured and Pierre dropped into the armchair by the fire after he had given her a square package bearing her name in Louis' thick, scrawled writing. It was sealed with red sealing-wax. Mirabel laid it aside without comment, and said, "Thank you for bringing it, Pierre. A sad loss to us all. I'm glad he didn't suffer. How is your grandmother?"

"Bearing up surprisingly well. She has decided to sell the house in Normandy and live at the holiday chalet in Switzerland. Paul and I have been unable to persuade her to come and live in England. She still has old Marie with her and I dare say she's right not to try to uproot herself at this stage of her life. She always loved the chalet, and they both spent more time there than in Normandy latterly. My grandfather died there."

"And you, Pierre? I'm quite out of touch."

Her dark blue eyes rebuked him, and he shrugged his shoulders with a wry little smile as he replied, "I spent a year or two abroad, then joined up with a friend who runs a fruit farm in Kent. Back to the land. Must be the old Valais farming streak coming out in me."

"Not far off, but you never called."

"I'm sorry, *Marraine*. I've become notoriously unsociable," he said lightly. "And to make matters worse, after neglecting you, I've come seeking your help."

"Why apologise for that, my dear? Your family and mine were friends long before you were born. What can I do for you?"

"It was my grandmother's suggestion that you might be able to help us. You knew that she and my grandfather adopted the orphaned grandchild of a friend?"

"I had heard, yes. That was the boy whose parents and grandparents were killed in an aeroplane disaster, wasn't it?"

"Yes. His grandfather lived a few weeks after the accident. My grandfather promised to take the boy, who was only four years old then. He's nine now. My grandmother feels that now she is on her own, and can't have many more years in front of her, Philippe should come to England and live with my brother. Paul and Janet are willing, but the boy isn't strong and has only just recovered from pneumonia. Needs exercise, fresh air. But Janet is a physiotherapist and works at their local hospital, and Paul's fully stretched wardening his stately home for the Trust. Belmont Hall. Our fruit farm adjoins it. What my grandmother suggests is that some capable English girl be found who could take charge of Philippe for this summer, improving his knowledge of English, until he can go to school next autumn. Once he's at school, Janet will be able to take care of him. He's not really strong enough to be pitched into a foreign school straight away, but Paul has found a good prep school willing to take him next September."

"I see," said Mirabel thoughtfully.

"My grandmother suggested that you might know of a suitable candidate for the job. She's very anxious to have a personal recommendation, young Philippe having suffered once before from an apparently good nanny who gave the child hell before my grandparents found her out. Janet doesn't know anybody suitable, and Paul and I are not entrusted with the task of finding someone, my grandmother being firmly convinced that any girl can hoodwink any man. You, with your large family connections, might be able to suggest somebody, she said. As it's only a temporary job, of course, it may not be easy, but my grandmother wants to see the candidate, have her over to spend a week or two in Switzerland before bringing Philippe to England, so that aspect might appeal to anyone who likes travelling."

"You must let me think about this, Pierre. One of my grandchildren is looking for another job. Antonia. I don't believe you've met her. What she has in mind, I don't quite know. But I'll consult the family, and give it some thought. It's my monthly family tea-party a week tomorrow. Will you join us? I might have some news for you by then. And if Antonia is interested, you can meet her then and judge for yourself."

"Splendid. And a thousand thanks, *Marraine*."

"Save your thanks, my dear. I may not be able to find any candidate for the post."

"I have great faith in your powers," said Pierre, smiling. "And what a large family circle you have to draw on! The Valais family is very thin on the ground compared with the Rainwoods."

"Yes, I'm very fortunate. Your grandfather, less so."

Pierre shrugged his shoulders, and said, half-mockingly, "We haven't your talent for domesticity, *Marraine*. Its joys somehow elude us. May I smoke?"

Mirabel gave her assent, and watched him as he lit a cigarette. The resemblance to his grandfather had grown even more striking during his absence, since to the same Roman nose, dark complexion, and black eyes, there was now added the same thinness of face where before the bones had been less prominent. Tallish, spare in build, he had something of his grandfather's panache in his personality, too. You always noticed Louis when he came into a room, no matter how crowded. And you would always notice Pierre. But there was one big difference. Louis' face had been expressive, his feelings there for all to read. Passionate, explosive, gay, angry — a man of intense feelings not disguised. But Pierre had always been more controlled and masked. That was a legacy from his English mother. To that cool assurance was now added an almost flippant, mocking air of which Mirabel did not approve.

Gwen brought in the tea-trolley and Mirabel apologised for her husband's absence.

"He had to attend a fund-raising committee meeting in the village," she said.

Pierre nodded, asked about his health and they exchanged polite platitudes until Mirabel said gently, "Your active work in the field of music. Have you given that up?"

"I do a certain amount of journalism in that field."

"The piano? You have a rich gift there, Pierre. No public work?"

"I still play occasionally, for myself. Earl Grey tea. Yours always tastes better than any other I have drunk. I always associate you with Earl Grey tea, fine china, and the scent of lavender."

"Very pretty associations, too," said Mirabel gravely.

He shot her a quick glance, then said with a quirky smile, "Allied to a very strong-minded lady, with a steely determination behind the diplomacy, it adds up to a formidable proposition. Your family are behaving well and causing no problems, I trust?"

"As I've seen so little of you during these past years, my dear, I don't intend to be deflected into discussing my family during the short time you will doubtless be here. I want to hear about you."

"What about me, *Marraine*? I'm in good health, reason-

ably sober, engaged in the financial intricacies of fruit
farming, and earning a modest living."

"Are you happy with your life?"

"Happiness is not in fashion. Gloom and doom are our
lot, it seems."

"Scepticism is destructive. And I'm not talking about
fashion. I'm concerned about an individual. My god-child.
I happen to be very fond of him."

Although her words were direct, unsparing, her voice
was gentle and her eyes compassionate. He lifted his hands
in an odd little gesture of resignation.

"I get along. I'm well occupied. Even enjoy myself sometimes. Should we expect more?"

"Claire's death has embittered you, my dear. Under-
standably. I'd hoped time would have helped in a more
constructive way."

"Now you mustn't make a tragic figure out of me. Sheer
sentimentality. I'm surprised at you, *Marraine*," he said
lightly.

"Sentimentality and sentiment are not the same. But
forgive me for probing. I can see it's unwelcome."

He stood up and looked down at her with a rueful smile.

"Now you're going to send me away feeling guilty."

"Must your visit be so short?"

"I was only a messenger today. At your tea-party, there
will be more time."

And more people to stand in the way of any intimate
exchanges, thought Mirabel. But she accepted defeat
gracefully.

"I shall look forward to seeing you there, Pierre, and I
hope I'll have something helpful to suggest about your
plans for Philippe. It was good of you to bring the package
instead of posting it."

"To be delivered into your hands. Those were my grandfather's instructions attached to the envelope. The men in
our family seem to have a foolish way of committing them-

selves wholeheartedly to lost causes. They can never quite give up."

And they are not good losers, thought Mirabel. The angry reproach in Louis' heart had lived on through the years, veiled but there in all their brief encounters, in the card he had sent her each Christmas, in the few letters she had received from him through the years. Always the little jab in the words. And it seemed that Pierre was the same. A bitter scepticism, a flippant mockery, they were his protest at the loss of his wife. And they had turned him into a stranger. Her heart ached for him although he had clearly shown that her sympathy was not wanted.

She stood in the porch watching him shoot away down the drive in a grey car at what she considered far too high a speed, then returned to the fire and opened the package. It contained all her letters, from the earliest days of their friendship, the paper yellowed now and the ink faded. There were two snapshots, one of her dressed in a white blouse and long dark skirt holding her bicycle, another of the two of them arm-in-arm in the driveway of the old Normandy farmhouse which was his home. Louis' mother had taken that, she remembered. It had been the last summer holiday they had spent together before her engagement to Charles Rainwood. Nearby, her back turned to them, oblivious, was the small hunched figure of the black cat, Manon. Manon, with the large amber eyes and the loudest purr in Normandy. There was no letter enclosing these relics of the past. Only two lines from Verlaine.

Qu'il était bleu, le ciel, et grand l'espoir !
L'espoir a fui, vaincu, vers le ciel noir.
                                        Louis.

2

Family Tea-Party

ANTONIA MENDYP, WALKING down the lane towards her grandmother's house, viewed the family tea-party with no great enthusiasm, and more than a little wariness. She had been asked to come an hour earlier than usual to discuss in greater detail a project mooted over the telephone a few days before which had singularly little appeal.

It was a sunny, breezy afternoon, and the lane was full of the scent of may blooming in the hedgerow. She would much have preferred to go off for a walk across the heath instead of having to answer the inevitable questions of her numerous relations on this, her first meeting with them since her return from her ill-fated job in Northumberland. She did not want to talk about yet another failure in her un-distinguished career, still less did she want to submit to her grandmother's deceptively gentle handling of the harrow across this stony ground. Today, she found herself unusually oppressed by a sense of failure and rejection. By nature eager and enthusiastic, the succession of failures was beginning to sap her confidence. A good gallop or walk across the heath would do far more to dispel this mood than her grandmother's tea-party.

She greeted her grandmother with her usual bright smile, however, and was conducted to the conservatory.

"We can be quiet here, before the others come, dear,"

said Mirabel, and Antonia obediently seated herself on a bench among the potted palms and exotic trailing plants while Mirabel sat in a straight-backed basket chair nearby. Here it comes, Antonia thought, and it did.

"I'm sorry that your job in Northumberland didn't last, Antonia. What went wrong? You were so enthusiastic about it, I remember. Some kind of zoo, wasn't it?"

"A private nature reserve, Grandma. The owner had great ideals, but little money. He'd bought this old manor house just for the land that went with it, and made a reserve of it. Birds and animals. He hoped to finance it by articles for newspapers and magazines about it, plus the savings he'd made in his business life. A sort of back-to-nature venture, you know," added Antonia, not sure that her grandmother was on her wave-length.

"And the practicalities defeated the ideals?"

"You might put it like that. I think he'd left it too late. He was middle-aged. He relied on me and one rather simple-minded youth to do the hard work. And he rarely had the money to pay our wages. A builder made him an offer for the land last month, and he accepted it. So that was that."

"I'm sorry. A disappointment for you. Perhaps you rushed in without examining it too closely," said Mirabel delicately.

"That's me," said Antonia cheerfully. "Destined to keep dashing up inviting paths only to find dead ends. I have a talent for it."

"You're young, dear. No bad thing to experiment."

" 'Character is destiny'. Somebody said that once. I was born an eager also-ran. But one success is enough in a family. Jonathan is doing brilliantly. He's in his element at Cambridge, and his teachers all predict a distinguished academic career for him. But of course Mother's told you all about that."

"Yes. Very gratifying," said Mirabel calmly. "But I don't

want to discuss Jonathan. Have you thought about my suggestion?"

"It doesn't sound up my street, Grandma. I'm not specially good with children, and certainly not clever enough to be a teacher. And I don't think I want to take on just another stop-gap."

"Have you anything more permanent in mind?"

"Not so far. I've only been home two weeks."

"You were always very good with Jonathan, and to speak English to a nine-year-old French boy so that he can become more fluent and not be handicapped at an English school is hardly a formidable teaching task. But I don't want to press you. I only throw it out as a suggestion. It would offer you a visit to Switzerland. I know your preference is for an out-of-door life, but this job would by no means confine you. The boy is delicate, needs building up with fresh air and exercise, I'm told. You would be working in beautiful country surroundings, and only until next September. If you're convinced that it is not for you, though, we'll say no more. Otherwise, you might care to discuss it further with Pierre Valais. He's coming to my tea-party today."

"Do I know him? The name rings a bell."

"The French side of my family had close ties with the Valais family. Pierre is my godson. His father and grand-father always kept in touch with me. Our paths have not crossed much in recent years, though, and it's unlikely that you've ever seen Pierre here."

"How does he come in to all this, then?"

Mirabel explained, adding, "He and his brother, Paul, have just returned from Switzerland after attending their grandfather's funeral. Pierre is going back to help his grandmother sort out business matters. Paul can't spare the time, since the season for visitors to Belmont Hall is getting under way."

"Do you know it? Belmont Hall."

"Only by hearsay. A fine eighteenth century house, with a famous collection of pictures and porcelain, set in grounds which I believe were laid out by Humphrey Repton."

"Rather formidable for a nine-year-old boy's background."

"Paul and his wife live at the lodge. That sounds like a car for the first of my arrivals. I'll leave it to Pierre to fill in the picture for you if you are interested. No harm in hearing what he has to say, anyway."

With most of Mirabel's children, grandchildren and great-grandchildren present at the long refectory table in the dining-room where a splendid tea was provided with the tastes of the younger generations in mind, the noise was considerable, and Antonia, seated next to her cousin, Nick, hoped that she could remain inconspicuous and untroubled by questions while she pondered her grandmother's proposition and took stock of Pierre Valais, seated at the far end of the table on the opposite side. He was laughing at something her cousin Susan had said to him, lifting up his hands in protest. Susan, pretty as a kitten, was looking up at him, her face tilted appealingly, exerting her considerable charm with some effect, it seemed. He made an impact, Antonia conceded. Intelligent face, assured, mature. Catching him a little later as he was glancing round the table with an air of faintly detached amusement, she detected a coolness that was off-putting; the sort of man with whom she always felt at a disadvantage.

"God, what a noise!" groaned Nick. "Why do we come?"

Antonia smiled at him. He was her favourite cousin.

"Must keep it up to the end now. Grandma's eighty-two, after all. Wouldn't do to upset the tradition at this late stage."

"Can't think how the old couple stand the racket. At that age, if I last that long, I shall be a recluse, opting for peace and quiet."

"A happy old bachelor, immersed in books. How do you cope with fame now? I saw a good review of your last biography."

"Hardly fame, my child. I get by."

"I bet you do," said Antonia, looking at the fair, handsome face of her cousin with admiration. "I envy you, Nick. You're so sure of the way you want to go. You lead the life you want to lead instead of being blown about by any wind that catches you, like most of us."

"Well, perhaps I was lucky in always knowing that I wanted to write. You sound a bit despondent. No joy in Northumberland?"

"No joy."

"Too bad. Fortify yourself with another cucumber sandwich."

That was the best of Nick, she thought. He never probed.

"I just seem to be running up blind alleys all the time."

"Away from what?" he asked casually.

Antonia blinked and side-stepped that one.

"A sense of inadequacy, perhaps," she said lightly.

"That's odd, coming from you, with your vitality and zest for life. I remember that summer we spent in Ireland. Quite exhausted me, that *joie de vivre* of yours," drawled Nick.

"Wasn't that a marvellous time? I'll never forget it. Magic, somehow."

"Nostalgia is very unproductive. Shouldn't indulge in it, if I were you."

She wondered whether there was more beneath his words than was apparent, then dismissed the thought that Nick could know anything about her long, hopeless love affair with Darrel Brynton which had haunted her ever since her encounter with him at the beginning of that summer in Ireland. Nobody knew. Not Darrel, who had only ever treated her as a child; not Jean, the girl he had married. Nobody. It lived a secret life in her heart. She had tried to forget it; had spent a year in Canada, thinking that distance might help. But the first sight of him after her return had only confirmed that it was not to be quenched. She had thrown herself into two jobs since then with all the enthusiasm she could muster, but they had come to nothing. Running away. Yes, she supposed that was what she had been doing for the past three years, with singularly little success.

Lost in recollections of Ireland, she let the noisy chatter of the tea-table wash over her until she came back to reality to find the remains of a cake on her plate which she had no recollection of eating, and, looking up, found Pierre Valais scrutinising her. Summing her up, she thought. Wondering whether she would fit the bill.

"As you know, Tonie," drawled Nick, "I never offer gratuitous advice — a pernicious habit. Perhaps quoting others is an equally pernicious habit, but I can't always resist that, and one little Spanish proverb comes to mind now. 'There are no birds in last year's nest.' Not a bad precept to keep in mind. I'm now going to plead an urgent engagement to Grandmama, and slide surreptitiously away. I can't stand this din any longer. If I were Robert, I'd put a muzzle on that child," he concluded, frowning at an eight-year-old boy who was shouting across the table at an aunt.

Mirabel, who had the knack of putting a cutting edge on her voice without raising it, intervened at that moment to reduce the boy to temporary silence, and Nick grinned.

"The old lady hasn't lost her touch, bless her! I shall have to brace myself to meet her sceptical eyes when I give her my excuse for leaving early. That formal courtesy of hers can be a devastating weapon. I shall creep out a guilty, shattered wreck. So long, Tonie. And good luck."

He drifted away. Antonia watched him hovering gracefully beside his grandmother, a quizzical little smile on his lips as he took his leave. Nothing, she thought, would ever make a guilty, shattered wreck out of Nick. She lifted her hand in smiling salute as he made a little grimace in her direction before slipping, almost unnoticed, through the door.

And then Uncle Peter's booming voice from across the table was asking her about her last job, and, with a sigh, she replied as briefly as she could, envying Nick his skill at disengaging himself.

After tea, with some of the Rainwood clan departing, others strolling round the garden or chatting in corners, Antonia was despatched by her grandmother to her grandfather's study at the back of the house, where she found Pierre Valais studying the bookshelves. He turned with a little smile.

"Antonia. You don't remember me?"

"No. We've never met before today, have we?" she asked, a little defensively.

"Not met, exactly. A near miss, you might say. About seven or eight years ago. Perhaps more. I can't remember precisely. I'd called to see your grandmother. As I was walking down the drive, you were running across the lawn, chasing a black and white dog. You streaked round the corner of the house like a comet."

"Gyp. He was always getting away from me, and had a passion for rolling in Grandma's precious herbaceous border. There was a rule that he was not to be allowed inside the front gate here unless on a lead, but he took some catching. He died some years ago. I'm surprised you remember."

"The red hair."

"Ah yes. My strident badge. Impossible to miss."

"It was very beautiful, in the sun. Flying free then," he added, eyeing the bow which now tied it back closely at the nape of her neck as though it was no improvement.

"My grandmother was telling me about this temporary job with your family, looking after a nine-year-old boy.

She thought I might like it, but I doubt whether I'm suitable. I've never had charge of children, except my own brother who is only two years younger than I am and was always good at looking after himself, anyway."

"So is Philippe, up to a point. All that is wanted is someone to keep him company and make him talk English all the time. From what I've seen of you, I think you'd be admirable. Young, lively, energetic. A good companion for a boy, I'd say. Especially one like Philippe, who's had rather a bad time and needs health and confidence restored."

"A bad time? In what way?"

"My grandparents employed a woman to look after him when my grandfather's health began to fail and my grandmother had as much as she could manage looking after him. The woman, kind and competent on the surface, turned out to be harsh, indeed something of a sadist. Philippe, rather an introspective little boy, didn't complain. Perhaps he was too frightened. My grandparents discovered it by chance, but not before a good deal of damage had been done. Added to which, Philippe adored my grandfather, and was very badly affected by his death. He's been ill. Pneumonia. And he isn't back to normal strength yet. So you see, we're very anxious to get the right sort of person to take him in hand this summer, and do a healing job. My grandmother is too old and frail. She thinks a new environment with younger people is desirable. But the changeover won't be easy for Philippe."

"I see. Poor little lad. He's to live with your brother, I believe."

"Yes. He and his wife have a comfortable home in the lodge of Belmont Hall. *Marraine* has told you about that?"

"*Marraine?*"

"Sorry. Your grandmother. She is my godmother, and I've always called her by that title since I was a kid. My case was the reverse of Philippe's. My French grandfather deplored the fact that his son settled in England after the war, married an English girl and made Englishmen of Paul and me. So when Grandfather came to see us, or we went to see him, he spoke nothing but French to us and insisted on us doing the same. And Mrs. Rainwood, he once informed me, was my *marraine*. It stuck. But tell me about yourself, Antonia. What have you been doing since I last saw the schoolgirl flashing across the lawn?"

If he thought she was going to give him her life story, he was very much mistaken, thought Antonia, not altogether liking his authoritative manner. He seemed to think she was still that schoolgirl he had once seen chasing a dog across the lawn. She spoke coolly with an assurance she was far from feeling, for in some odd way this man with the shrewd dark eyes disconcerted her.

"Oh, I spent a year in Canada on a ranch, where they bred and trained horses. Then I had a private job in Surrey, teaching a disabled girl to ride, and I've been working up in Northumberland for the past few months, in a nature reserve."

"You like to keep moving, then."

"Yes. And to be out-of-doors. There must be a lot of people more suitable for the job you have in mind than I am."

"Well, it's not really a job in the ordinary sense of the word, is it? Just stepping in for a few summer months to help a small boy to get launched on a new life in a foreign country. No more than a short interlude for you, with a visit to Switzerland thrown in. Could be of enormous benefit to the boy, though. We would pay well, and you would have no expenses, but I doubt whether that aspect matters a great deal to you. According to your grandmother, you are singularly unworldly."

"Just a simple-minded, outdoor, horsy type," said Antonia drily, well aware of her grandmother's less than enthusiastic attitude towards horse-lovers, and her view that such obsessions should not outlast adolescence.

The black eyes regarding her gleamed mischievously, but his face was solemn as he said,

"I was left to form my own judgment, but my grandfather's faith in your grandmother was such that I would never question any recommendation she made. And she told me just now that if you could be persuaded, you would be just the person to take the chill out of Philippe's life because you had a warm vitality that was infectious."

"Flattery will get you nowhere, Mr. Valais."

"Pierre. And have you ever known your grandmother to flatter?"

"Never."

"Nor I," he said ruefully, and Antonia smiled in spite of herself.

"She has what my cousin, Nick, terms a delicate astringency. There's not one member of our family, young or old, who doesn't respect it."

"Well, what about this proposition? Unless you've definitely decided it's not for you, I suggest that you see Paul and Janet, and then if you're all happy about it, you return with me to Switzerland and meet my grandmother and the boy before you finally decide."

She sensed an impatience in him, although the polite façade held, as though he was anxious to get this chore over. She considered him, her head on one side.

"One thing puzzles me a little. Why are you doing this and not your brother and his wife? They, after all, are the people most involved."

"Quite simple. My grandfather, before he died, discussed Philippe's future with my grandmother, and was emphatic about seeking Mrs. Rainwood's help in finding a suitable person to help Janet and Paul break Philippe into his new life. They had both been shocked at their own lamentable failure to see through that sadistic woman, and in my grandfather's opinion, Mirabel Rainwood would never have made such a mistake. Paul hardly knows your grandmother.

I, as her godchild, know her better. The first approach, therefore, seemed best made by me."

"I understand."

"Also, my grandfather asked me to play my part, too, in keeping an eye on Philippe, since the child has no relatives of his own. The old man was devoted to the boy, and felt it his duty to his old friend to treat him as his own. Philippe's grandfather and mine were in the French Resistance movement together during the war. Such ties mean a lot."

Again there was a rough edge of impatience in his voice, as though he was tired of this interview. He had turned away from her, and was standing with one hand slowly tapping on the mantelpiece as he studied the old-fashioned marble clock. He didn't want this duty, she thought. The tick of the clock was now the only sound in the room. In the large mirror over the fireplace she looked at their reflections as though at a picture, a sudden feeling of unreality taking hold. A dark man, head bent, with a brooding expression. A girl with red hair, pale skin, slender and only a few inches shorter than he. What had they to do with each other, these strangers? Then he looked up and caught her gaze in the mirror, and she shivered and walked across to the window. Outside, two young Rainwoods were crouched over the garden pool, watching the goldfish. She felt uneasy, repelled by something dark and smouldering behind the urbane exterior of Pierre Valais, and at the same time impatient with herself for not being able to give a plain yes or no to a perfectly straightforward proposition.

"Well?" he asked, obviously not going to waste any more time in persuasion.

Behind this vaguely menacing man stood the lonely figure of a nine-year-old boy. A summer interlude, no more, when she could be of use. She turned and said abruptly,

"How do I get to Belmont Hall?"

"Do you drive?"

"No."

"I'll meet you at Kingsford Station. Are you free on Monday?"

She was, and he gave her directions; an easy train journey from her local station, involving one change. He would meet her off the train which arrived at Kingsford at eleven o'clock.

"Monday's a quiet day at Belmont Hall as far as visitors are concerned, and Paul will be delighted to show you over the place, whatever you decide about the job," he said.

And so it was left. She returned to the party, and did not see him again. By the time she had strolled round the garden with her grandfather, he had gone.

3

Belmont Hall

THE SUN WAS shining out of a cloudless blue sky when
Antonia walked out of Kingsford Station on Monday
morning to see Pierre at the wheel of a long grey car,
awaiting her. They said little during the short drive through
lanes edged with the white lacy flowers of wild parsley
backed by hedgerows bright with the first tender young
leaves of summer. Nearing their destination, the lane narrowed and climbed on a twisting course up hill until they
emerged on open park-land. Pierre turned the car through
wide gates and up a long tree-lined avenue. At the end was
a large space cleared among trees for a car park. They
skirted this, and the massive, grey stone building that was
Belmont Hall lay before them in a landscaped setting of
lawns and trees and terraces, serenely beautiful in the May
sunshine. At Antonia's exlamation of admiration, Pierre
said, "Eighteenth century. The interior lives up to the
exterior, too. Magnificent furniture, a collection of Sèvres
and Dresden china, a picture gallery with works by Gains-
borough and Reynolds, as well as some good work from
Dutch and French artists of the seventeenth and eighteenth
centuries. A treasure-house. Paul's the man to show it all
to you, if you're interested. It's his period."

"He must love his job."

"Yes. It's his whole life."

"Has he had the job long?"

"For the past four years he's been in charge. He was an assistant for some time before that. I brought you round this way so that you could see the house and grounds first, but the lodge where Paul and Janet live is at the other end of the estate with its own entrance farther down the lane."

"Helping them to keep one foot in the present, perhaps. With this grandiose background, it would be easy just to live in the past."

"Why not? The present isn't all that attractive."

They were following a gravelled road running below the terrace of the house. To their left, smooth lawns dotted with fine old trees sloped down to a belt of shrubs and woodland.

"Is that the boundary?" she asked. "The woodland?"

"No. There's another grassy walk beyond that, known as Poets' Walk, overlooking the river valley. The river forms the present boundary, but the land on the other side was once part of the estate. It was sold off for farming early in this century. The land my partner and I farm was part of it."

By now they were skirting an area of rough pasture, left to nature, which at that time of the year put on a show which rivalled the beauty of all the landscaping and gardening skill which had been lavished for so many years on the land surrounding the house. The tall meadow grasses mingled with buttercups and daisies and countless wild flowers which Antonia could not identify at the quickened pace at which Pierre was driving. She thought she saw cowslips there, and red ragged robin.

"An English meadow on a sunny May day. It takes some beating," she said.

"Yes. Its only rival is an Alpine meadow about a month later. Hard put to it to choose between them."

"Meadows like this, unsprayed and left to nature, are few and far between in England now, though. Are they

less progressive in the Swiss Alps?" asked Antonia with a
hint of acid which surprised him and brought an appre-
ciative smile to his lips. A touch of the old lady there, he
thought.

"The flowers bloom freely until they are all cut for hay
for the cattle. You can enjoy them during late May and
early June, then it's the knife."

"A nice varied diet for the cows, then."

"If you come to Switzerland, you'll be in time to see the
display before the execution."

"You're making it all terribly attractive. This beautiful
place, and now the Swiss Alps held out to tempt me. You
knew if you got me here that I couldn't refuse, didn't
you?"

"I thought you might find the set-up persuasive," he
said smoothly.

"I might not suit the other parties, though."

"I've told you. You under-estimate the reputation of
Mirabel Rainwood in our family. It would be like handing
the tablets back to Moses to turn down a recommendation
from her."

He drew up outside a square, red-brick house, and a tall,
fair-haired man emerged and walked down the path to
greet them. He had a thin, ascetic face, and wore heavy
horn-rimmed glasses. Pierre introduced them. Paul Valais
bore no resemblance at all to his brother, in looks or
manner, she thought. A quiet voice, a friendly smile.
Nothing smouldering or moody or mocking there. She
found him reassuring. He apologised for his wife's absence.
She would be home to lunch. He had coffee ready for them.
After that, he was due at the Hall. Would they like to
walk across with him? Pierre could show her over the Hall
while he attended to some business there.

Over coffee, and during the walk back to Belmont Hall,
Antonia was aware that for all his easy, quiet manner, Paul
was subjecting her to an unobtrusive examination, and

decided that there was one quality which the brothers shared, after all; a natural authority. Paul's was more under-stated than Pierre's, and therefore more readily acceptable, but there, all the same.

When they arrived at the Hall, Pierre declined to take Antonia over it.

"That's best left to you, Paul. You do conducted tours so much better than I. There's too much to see in what's left of this morning, anyway. I'll take Antonia round the grounds. She'll enjoy that more than listening to me as a guide, I am sure."

Written off as an outdoor type, incapable of appreciating fine painting, architecture, or historic treasures, she thought as Paul arranged to meet them on the terrace in an hour's time and disappeared into the Hall.

By now, there were several people strolling about the grounds. The next conducted tour round Belmont Hall, according to the notice she had seen on a board outside the main entrance, was at three o'clock.

"There are no un-guided tours round the Hall?" she asked.

"No. Too much valuable stuff in there. Paul shares the guiding with another man."

"A big responsibility for your brother."

"Yes. He has a good staff of assistants, though. All very keen."

"Where do they live?"

"In the flats over the old stables. There's more accommodation over the refreshment room they built behind the stable block, too. Gardeners and cleaners come in from the village. The chief gardener lives in a cottage just outside the eastern boundary."

"A costly business, keeping it going."

"There's an endowment. Not enough, of course, for present day costs. But the visitors come in ever-increasing numbers, and the refreshment side makes a healthy profit.

It's Paul's major preoccupation, though. Balancing the budget."

He led her through a formal rose garden, along a deep and long herbaceous border, and then across the lawn towards the woodland. She stopped to read some of the small plaques at the foot of individual trees in the lawn, giving the names of the famous people who had planted them, and the dates. Pierre, not inclined to linger, strolled on. She caught him up at the woodland. This was shallow in depth, and when she stepped out on to the wide grassy walk beyond, she gasped with pleasure at the view of the river valley and the wooded slopes on the other side.

"Where is your farm?"

"Out of sight from here. Round the bend in the river. You can just see the fruit blossom through the trees from that bay."

At intervals all along the walk were paved bays, each holding a stone figure on a plinth and a seat placed to take full advantage of the view. On each plinth was carved a verse, and these Antonia studied with some interest. About half way along, Pierre said, "I'll leave you to explore the rest of the walk on your own, and to read, learn and inwardly digest the rhyming couplets which I find patronisingly tedious. I'd have chosen lines from different poets myself."

"Such as?"

"I need notice of that question. You have about twenty minutes."

He leaned on the stone balustrade of the bay and lit a cigarette. Dismissed, Antonia tightened her lips and directed a far from benign look in his direction, but he had turned his back and was gazing across the valley. She went on her way, annoyed at being peremptorily dismissed like a child who had taken up too much of his time. Reading every inscription as she went, she had to admit, however, that she shared Pierre's lack of enthusiasm for the element of moral rectitude evident in each of them, so that the cumulative effect by the time she came to the end of the Poets' Walk was of a long lecture from a humourless judge. But what a beautiful view it was, she thought, as she leaned on the sun-warmed stone balustrade of the last bay and gazed across the valley. Far more uplifting to the spirit than the moralising couplets.

As she walked back, the figure of Pierre Valais leaning on the balustrade was as still as any of the stone figures on the plinths. Drawing near, the grim, bitter expression of that brooding face shocked her. The grass softened her footsteps and she was beside him before he heard her. Instantly, his face was masked, and he said lightly, "Well, do you feel better for that?"

"Wordsworth. He would have been my choice."

"Ah, the nature-lover.

      ' My heart leaps up when I behold
      A rainbow in the sky.' "

She flushed at his flippant tone. He evidently could not take her seriously. It was an attitude from which she had often suffered before. An ingenuous, naïve child. It rubbed a sore place.

"We'd better get back to the Hall," she said curtly.

He gave her a quick, sidelong glance.

"What's wrong?"

"I don't like cynics."

"Your directness is refreshing, Antonia. Forgive me. As a matter of fact, I share your regard for Wordsworth. You like poetry?"

"Yes. That surprises you?" she added with a gentle irony not lost on him, for there was a gleam of amusement in his eyes as he replied, in equally dulcet tones,

"Why should it? I would guess that your taste is for

the romantic rather than the classic, for the lyrics of the
lovers of life rather than the waste-landers. Correct?"

"Yes."

"As it should be, too."

She smiled and said no more, willing to let the challenge
rest as a mood of happiness swept over her. In this beautiful place on a sunny May morning, why should she be so
touchy about his attitude? He had every right to prefer his
own thoughts to her company, and it was foolish and
unreasonable of her to blame him for rubbing a sore place
which an unrequited love affair had created. The growing
list of failure and frustration in both her emotional and her
working life had, she knew, induced in her a touchiness
foreign to her until the last few months. It was time she
snapped out of it. This new opportunity, although only
of a temporary nature, was beginning to look promising.
A spark of excitement at the prospect was beginning
to glow. Perhaps this time, she would make a success of
it. Achieve something worth while. And forget Darrel
Brynton.

Her impressions of Paul's wife did nothing to dim her
spirits. Janet Valais, trim, dark, business-like, had a friendly
manner combined with a frankness that suited Antonia.
And by the end of that luncheon, it seemed that Antonia
had made an equally favourable impression.

"You're just the reassuring type of person Philippe
needs," Janet said, pouring the coffee. "Between us, we
should be able to put him on his feet again. He was always
a serious, introspective boy, but that diabolical woman has
driven him right into himself. I was shocked when I saw
him. And I hate to see fear in a child's eyes."

"I can't think why my grandmother didn't spot it
before," said Paul.

"She was too taken up with looking after your grandfather, once his health began to fail. No, he's the one I
should have thought would have spotted that something

was wrong. He loved Philippe. For your grandmother, I fancy it was a question more of duty than love. And duty hasn't got the insight of love."

"Grandmama," said Pierre drily, "is a rather dried nut, anyway. Not given to sentiment. A stickler for duty, though. She's concerned to do her best for Philippe, since it was Grandfather's wish."

"I hope she'll think I'm suitable, then," said Antonia.

"You hope? Then you want to take it on, after all?" asked Pierre, that same gleam of amusement in his black eyes.

"Yes," replied Antonia smoothly. "It's more appealing than I thought at first. It's quite different from anything I've ever undertaken before, and I would never have thought of it for myself."

"Have you been conned into this, then?" asked Janet.

"Between my grandmother and Pierre, I rather fancy I have."

"Pierre's a skilful operator, and from what I've heard of the formidable Mirabel Rainwood, I'd say you hadn't much chance. Our good fortune," concluded Janet with a warm smile.

"How long are you going to need to clear up the business matters over there, Pierre?" asked Paul.

"Two or three weeks at the most, I hope."

"Sorry I've had to leave it all to you, but you're better at that sort of thing than I am, anyway."

While the two men discussed business matters arising from their grandfather's death, Janet drew Antonia outside.

"Let's walk round the meadow before I go back. One or two things I'd like to fill in. First, don't let Grandma Valais put you off. She can be off-putting, as I know only too well. A dried-up old nut, as Pierre said. But all right, if you know how to take her. Don't expect anything warm or gracious, though. She's a bit chilling whoever you are, but to Mirabel Rainwood's granddaughter, she might ration

even that very small amount of warmth she manages to
exude towards the rest of us."

"But Pierre said that anyone Mirabel Rainwood put
forward would be accepted."

"True. Grandfather Valais drilled his wife thoroughly
in that respect. But there's more to it than that. Did you
know that Grandfather Valais was once passionately in love
with your grandmother?"

"Heavens, no!" said Antonia, startled. "Not the sort of
thing Grandma would ever talk about."

"Well, it was a love affair he never grew out of. He
always thought she had betrayed him by marrying Charles
Rainwood, and although it sounds far-fetched and highly
romantic, in a sense he never stopped loving her, or
loving his memory of her. They didn't see much of each
other after she married. He was a passionate man, Paul's
grandfather. Felt everything deeply. All his emotions
involved."

"How hard to imagine it, so long ago! I guess Grandma
was a stunner."

"And Grandpa Valais, too. Anyway, I had all this from
Paul. The old man wasn't as reticent as your grandmother,
and both Paul and Pierre were aware of this old family
romance that came to naught, and so, of course, was
Grandma Valais. I don't know how long it was before
she knew, but that sort of obsession isn't easily hidden from
a wife. I guess she lived with the spectre of Mirabel Rainwood most of her married life."

"Then why should she agree to see me? If I were her, I
wouldn't want any reminders."

"She's an old lady now. Seventy-nine. Your grandmother
is what?"

"Eighty-two."

"The blood runs cold. Old fires die. It ceases perhaps in
the end to matter."

"But it's changed you, all the same," said Antonia slowly.

"Past history. I shouldn't have told you, but I wanted you to be forewarned, in case the welcome is cool. Don't be put off. She'll want to do what's best for Philippe. Pierre's quite right there. Mirabel Rainwood may not be a name beloved by his grandmother, but her help was sought and her judgment will be respected."

"Well, thanks for preparing me. Who would have thought it? A romantic legend in the family. I shall keep it to myself, though. My grandmother believes in a mannerly reticence in all such matters."

"We could certainly do with a bit more of it nowadays, at any rate. I must be off. I'm due at the hospital at three o'clock. I'm so relieved and glad that you're willing to take this on, Antonia. I feel, and I hope you do, that you'll fit in very happily with us. I had doubts about the whole project. Whether Paul and I were suitable people in the first place. We're both absorbed in our work, you know. And having no children of our own ..." She was silent for a moment, then went on briskly, "Well, there was nobody else who could offer the boy a home, so we must do our best. The worst part, the first few months, will be enormously helped if you come, though, so I'll be praying nothing puts you off."

"I think Pierre will see to that. Between him and Grandma, you know, I've been nicely managed."

Janet smiled and shook her head.

"No, you're too independent ever to be managed against your wishes, I'm sure, though I'm not underrating Pierre's managing ability."

Antonia elected to join the party being conducted over Belmont Hall that afternoon by a uniformed guide, and could hardly take in the wealth of furniture, paintings, porcelain and tapestries housed there. She would have liked to linger, taking it in more slowly, and hoped that she would be allowed to go over it on her own some time if she came to live there that summer. When she expressed this wish to Pierre, as he was driving her to the station, he said,

"Get Paul to take you over once or twice first. He knows and loves every article there. You'll learn a lot from him, which will add to your enjoyment if you're ever let loose there on your own, but Paul's pretty strict on that point. He's the custodian. And the contents are priceless, and in many cases fragile."

"So much that's beautiful. You just want to stand and stare, not be shepherded along. Especially, for me, the picture gallery. Those Dutch landscape paintings. I could forget time and lose myself in those."

"I dare say you'll get a special dispensation if you're that reverent," said Pierre.

"I hope so."

"Looking forward to your summer here, then?"

"Machiavelli. Who wouldn't?"

"I'll book your flight to Zurich tomorrow. It's a train journey of about an hour from there. How soon can you be ready? By the end of the week?"

She agreed, and he left her at the station, acceding to her request not to wait for the train with unflattering promptitude. With her mind an excited jumble of reflections on the beauty of Belmont Hall, the coming journey to Switzerland, the prospect of facing a formidable old lady, and the frightened, unhappy boy who was the cause of this sudden change of direction in her life, she all but forgot to change trains and tumbled out of her carriage as the train was starting to move again.

It was dark when she walked up the lane from her home station, but the sky was clear and the moon cast a chequered pattern of silver through the branches of the overhanging trees. The air was fresh and cool, and fragrant with the scent of may blossom. She listened for the nightingale known to sing from a neighbouring coppice, but the call of an owl was all she heard.

Only two days ago, she had gone to Grandma Rainwood's

family tea-party in a grey mood of dejection, certain that the tentative proposal for this temporary job was wildly unsuitable and held no appeal for her. Now, it seemed to offer an exciting challenge. And not the least part of that challenge was Pierre Valais, who had handled it all so cleverly. Whatever was in store, the mood of failure and dejection was now swept away by the prospect before her. This time, she thought, it would be different. Not another dead-end of useless effort. Something absorbing and worthwhile that would keep her thoughts from sliding nostalgically back to golden days in Ireland and Darrel Brynton.

Her steps quickened as she saw the light in the porch of her home. She would have much to tell her parents. Poor, long-suffering parents, she thought, half humorously. Always hearing about enthusiastic new ventures that would take her far from home, and having her back in due course with clipped wings. Now they were about to hear of another one. They always listened patiently, but without much enthusiasm, and, of late, a definite note of scepticism could be detected in her mother's response, and small wonder. This time, though, it really would be different. It must be.

4

A Champagne Evening

THE FLIGHT TO Zurich was uneventful and disappointingly
dull, for they flew on a very early plane through cloud
most of the way, but the sun was shining brilliantly when
they boarded the train for Lakendorf, and the Swiss
countryside of meadow and lake and mountains unfolded
before Antonia's eager eyes.

Pierre, an unflurried, efficient travelling companion,
read a magazine until the last part of the journey, when
the train ran along the side of a vast lake. On the far side
against a blue sky the distant Alpine peaks stood out, their
snowy crests clearly defined, and Pierre put his magazine
aside and named some of them for her.

"You know them well. Have you done any climbing?"
she asked.

"In my teens, when we spent family holidays with the
grandparents. Then we switched our enthusiasm to skiing
and came out in the winter instead of summer. They were
good holidays. Seems a long time ago."

"How colourful and pretty it all is!"

"Tame, after Canada?"

"No. Friendly and inviting. I like it."

He smiled and picked up his magazine again. Antonia
gazed out of the window at the pretty little lake-side
villages, where the deep-eaved wooden houses had ornately

carved balconies gay with geraniums, neat little gardens, and artistically stacked wood in the form of walls or porches round the doors to remind one that winter was harsh and all was not sunshine and flowers. But on that day of early summer, the landscape could not have been happier, and she felt her heart lift to its appeal. Small, tree-shaded squares in the middle of the villages looked peaceful and inviting, with gaily painted little tables and chairs set out to encourage the passer-by to linger. Along the lake-side promenade there were brightly painted seats, too, and everywhere there was colour to delight her eyes. The greeny-blue water of the lake, the green wooded slopes of mountains coming down to the lake, the higher snow-capped mountains in the background, white steamers on the lake. And flowers wherever space could be found. Even the stone water trough with its running tap in the centre of one of the lake-side village squares had its tap-stand crowned with geraniums.

How I love colour, thought Antonia, in a state of intoxication at this panorama, unable to conceive how Pierre could sit there engrossed in a magazine while all this was passing him by. She turned to say so, then stopped on the brink of speech, frozen by the wintry bleakness of his expression as he read. His lips were compressed, and his lean face had a clenched look, as though withstanding great pain. He was miles away, she thought, in a tortured world of his own, and she turned back to the window, startled by this glimpse of naked feeling on the face of a man who had hitherto displayed no more than a faintly mocking urbanity, punctured now and again by a barely controlled impatience. She had thought him singularly devoid of feeling. Now she realised that she knew nothing of him, and wished that she had questioned her grandmother more about him, for in spite of his undoubtedly off-putting aspects, she found him interesting and challenging.

They had the compartment to themselves, and silence

ruled between them until the train was running through the outskirts of Lakendorf, when Antonia said, "How far is the chalet from here?"

He was stowing the magazine into his briefcase, and she had a sufficient glimpse of its cover to see that it was a magazine devoted to music. That raw, strangely shocking expression on his face was now masked again, and his voice held its customary note of cool detachment as he replied, "Only about three miles. The first village along the lake from Lakendorf. Should be a taxi waiting for us."

Their somewhat breathless drive from the station brought them quickly to their destination, a large wooden chalet on the outskirts of a village similar to the other lake-side villages which had so charmed her on the train journey. The same deep eaves to the chalets, the ornately carved balconies, geraniums and marguerites in the window boxes. As with the other villages, too, there were no rows of chalets there, just a scattering up the slopes from the lake in a pleasing informality, with plenty of space, green meadow or woodland, in between.

So far, thought Antonia as Pierre paid the taxi-driver, all was most reassuring. Now for Madame Valais, and a possible flaw in this idyllic picture. And even as she squared her shoulders and braced herself, the door of the chalet opened and a white-haired, rosy-cheeked, plump little woman stood there, smiling broadly. Antonia's relief at the thought that Pierre and Janet had misled her about the forbidding qualities of Madame Valais was short-lived, however, for after Pierre had been warmly greeted and embraced, he introduced the little woman as Marie, and Antonia realised that she was the housekeeper. Although she had greeted Pierre in a quick babble of French, she spoke in careful English to Antonia, and led them through the hall into a large, sunny sitting-room with windows looking out across the lake. In an armchair by the window sat a small, grey-haired woman who rose stiffly as they came in. She was thin and her shoulders were bowed, but the dark eyes were as bright as wet prunes in the dried-up sallow face.

"*Mon cher,*" she said, embracing Pierre.

"*Grand'mere. Comment cela va-t-il?*"

"I am well, thank you, Pierre. During your visit, I have made a rule. We will speak only in English. To help Philippe. And make our visitor feel at home," she added, turning to Antonia.

Pierre introduced them, and Antonia felt herself subjected to a penetrating scrutiny.

"So you are Mirabel Rainwood's grand-daughter."

"One of several."

"Yes. The Rainwood family is a large one now, I hear. I hope your grandmother is well. It is many, many years since I saw her."

Marie brought in coffee and Antonia responded to the polite probings from Pierre's grandmother with a cheerful frankness which seemed to go down well, for the old lady began to unbend a little.

"Where is Philippe?" asked Pierre as he accepted a second cup of coffee.

"I sent him for a short walk as the morning is so fine. He is still rather weak after his illness. He is due back shortly."

"How is he taking the prospect of life in a new country? Better than when I was last here?"

"He says very little. He is unnaturally bottled up about it. I can't seem to reach him. He is afraid, I think. You, I feel, will reassure him, Antonia. So different from that other woman who still, I fancy, haunts him. However, let us see how you get on during the next two weeks."

"Is he to be in my care?" asked Antonia.

"No. Marie will continue to look after him. I would like you to gain his confidence, if you can. See if you can establish a good relationship. Then, if you are willing and I am satisfied, Philippe can go back with you and Pierre and start a new life. I am only sorry that Janet cannot give up her work to look after him," concluded Madame Valais with a severe expression which made it clear that she did not view careers for married women in a favourable light.

"Once he gets to a good prep school, he'll be all right. Janet's home in the evenings and at weekends," observed Pierre.

"Well, we shall see. Meanwhile, Antonia, I hope you will enjoy your stay with us. The business matters which Pierre is seeing to for me will not occupy all his time. I am sure he will be pleased to show you round and do what he can to make your visit agreeable."

"Thank you," said Antonia, then turned as the door opened and a thin, white-faced boy with a mop of black hair hovered in the doorway.

"Ah, Philippe. Come in, my dear," said Madame Valais, "and meet Miss Mendyp."

He had evidently been well drilled, for he marched up to Antonia and gave her a stiff little bow, but avoided looking at her face as he murmured, *"Bon jour, mademoiselle."*

And for the remainder of that first, rather strained day, Philippe avoided looking directly at Antonia, and met all her overtures with a kind of tense politeness. Only once, while she was talking to Pierre, she caught the boy looking at her across the room with an odd expression which both touched and shocked her. It combined fear with a kind of desolate stoicism. He seemed to her an extraordinarily lonely child. His relationship with Madame Valais was one of formal politeness. With Marie he was quiet and passive, and towards Pierre he exhibited a tentative approach, accepting his casual friendliness with a shy wariness. It would not be easy, she thought, to find the way through this boy's defences.

Something of Philippe's desolation stole up on her, too, as the day wore on. The boy was sent early to bed, and Madame Valais, with little finesse, prodded Antonia about her life. The year in Canada, the abortive jobs since. It hardly added up to an impressive recital, she felt, but the old lady nodded her head with judicial approval and said, "Interesting experiences. It is good not to get into a rut when you are young. To see something of the world. When you are married, it will be different."

"Oh, I think that's most unlikely."

"Unlikely that you'll be married, or unlikely that it will be different?" asked Pierre.

"Unlikely that I shall marry."

"And how old are you, Antonia?" asked Madame Valais.

"Twenty-one."

"So. You will soon grow out of making such foolish pronouncements. Now, I am tired. I shall go to bed. There is a Viennese concert and dancing at the Kursaal in the town tonight, Pierre. If Antonia is not too tired after the journey, why not take her? This is a dull household for young people just now."

"Are you tired?" asked Pierre coolly.

They had started early that morning from Heathrow, but Antonia, far from feeling tired, had a sudden fierce urge to escape for a few hours from the probing eyes of Pierre's grandmother, from the problem presented by Philippe, from the recollection of the naked pain on Pierre's face in the train that morning, from her own memories of Darrel. It seemed to her then that they were all haunted by past losses, she, Pierre, Philippe, Madame Valais.

"I'm not a bit tired," she said, her eyes sparkling suddenly as she sensed Pierre's reluctance. "I'd love to go."

He met the challenge in her face with a wry smile as he said, "Well, perhaps I could do with a little frivolity myself. I'll telephone for a taxi. Can you be ready in half an hour?"

"Try me," she said, and flashed a grateful smile at Pierre's grandmother before slipping out of the room.

She had a quick shower, slipped into a jade green silk jersey dress, tied her hair back at the nape of her neck with a matching ribbon, slipped into a light coat and joined Pierre in the hall with half a minute to spare. He looked at her with approval. It was, she thought, the first time he had become aware of her as a person in her own right.

"Nice work. Your enthusiasm is infectious. Let's go."

The sun was sinking as they drove along the twisting road through the woods. She caught glimpses of the lake below them through the trees, and regretted the speed of the taxi, and said so.

"Out of place in this beautiful peaceful setting. I feel we should be proceeding gently in a horse-drawn carriage," she said.

"A romantic? They cater for people like you in the town, you know. Trips in horse-drawn carriages are very popular with tourists."

"I refuse to be quenched by your scepticism."

"Quite right, too. I'd hate to see you quenched. At your age, I had my romantic moments, too."

"Old, old man. Just pretend to be young this evening."

"I'll do my best," he said gravely, his eyes dancing. "Any helpful suggestions?"

But she took his flippant words seriously and thought for a moment before she turned to him and said,

"Shall we, just for tonight, wipe out all the past, put the future out of our minds, and enjoy a few stolen hours with free minds and hearts?"

He looked at her, surprised.

"Have you things to forget, then?"

"Haven't we all?" she replied lightly.

"I took you for the most lively, carefree young thing I'd ever seen," he said slowly, searching her face. "A love affair gone wrong?"

"The formula for this evening is enjoyment of the moment, remember."

"At your command. A champagne evening it shall be."

They were driving along the main thoroughfare of Lakendorf, a wide road, gay with open-air cafés, inviting shops and impressive hotels, and liberally bedecked with flowers in window boxes, in tubs outside the cafés, and in the forecourts of hotels. And far away in the background, but dominating the town, the massive snowy summit of a mountain reflecting the pink afterglow of the sun.

"What else could it be but a champagne evening in this fairyland town?" declared Antonia, carried away by the potent spell of the place.

"You're pulling years off my shoulders every minute," said Pierre, laughing, as the taxi drew up outside the gates of the park which was the setting for the Kursaal.

Arm-in-arm, they walked through the park, past carpet bedding of geraniums and begonias that glowed in the gathering dusk like rich jewels, towards the high jets of the fountain that played in the centre of a large lake. Antonia could feel the cool spray on her cheeks as they walked round it. Beyond the lake lay the massive stone building of the Kursaal, itself evoking further the fairytale atmosphere of the surroundings with its turrets and massive arched entrance.

As they approached the building, Pierre stopped and turned her round to look back at the mountain peak, where the last pink glow was fading from the snowfields.

"It has everything, this place, hasn't it?" he said, and Antonia agreed, conscious of his firm hands on her shoulders.

And when the afterglow had vanished from the mountain peak to leave it stark and cold, with a timeless, deathly serenity, Antonia gave another gasp of delight as floodlights sprang to life round them, illuminating the fountain jets, the flower-beds, and turning the stone of the Kursaal to a warm gold. And just then, the sound of music reached them.

"Well, is Cinderella ready for the ball?" asked Pierre.

"It's all a dream. I hope I don't wake up."

"I'll try to see that you don't."

The ballroom of the Kursaal was fringed with tables and chairs where people were drinking and chatting and watching the dancing in the central area. The orchestra played the Viennese music with the authentic lilt, and earned Pierre's approval as they sipped the champagne he had insisted on ordering before they joined the dancers, although Antonia's toes were tapping all the time they were seated at their table and she could hardly bear to wait so long.

"I'll gladly waltz," he said, as he stood up at last, "but I decline to gallivant round in a polka. Shakes up the champagne too much. You must choose a more juvenile partner for that. I may be shedding years fast, but not that fast."

She smiled and went into his arms for the 'Gold and Silver' waltz. He was a good partner in this style of dancing, combining firmness of control with a certain panache, and Antonia, who loved the old fashioned dances, was soon dancing with him as though they had practised together for years. There was no past, she thought. No future. Just a fairytale ballroom, gay, lilting music, the firm hold of a partner whose dark good looks and challenging personality were all part of the magic.

She had never expected Pierre to throw himself into the mood of that gay Viennese evening, or indeed had thought him capable of doing so. She had experienced the mocking, flippant Pierre Valais, and the tense, impatient version with its hint of hidden passion, but the gaiety and charm with which he indulged her mood that evening both surprised and delighted her, and sent her already high spirits rocketing away into starry space.

When she returned to their table after dancing a polka with a large, blond Austrian holiday-maker, he said, "That chap's been eyeing you for some time. Not surprising, since you're sparkling like that crystal chandelier. Do you want me to make myself scarce and give him a chance?"

"Certainly not. Don't spoil your act of gallantry this evening by such a suggestion. You're playing the part so beautifully."

"Could gallantry go further than such self-sacrifice?"

"I shall be charitable and assume that you're not seeking a very righteous excuse for a get-out, and assure you that I would rather dance with you than with that fair giant. He's heavy on his feet, and hasn't really got the knack. And if I have any more champagne, I shall lose the knack myself," she said, moving her glass away as Pierre went to top it up.

"Let's drink a toast," he said, lifting his glass. "To Antonia's land of make-believe."

She smiled at him over her glass.

"Confess, you're enjoying it, too."

"Amazingly, yes. Haven't felt so young and light-hearted for years. How right your grandmother was to recommend you to us! You'll be marvellous for young Philippe. He's been with old people too long."

"I don't think it will be quite as simple as that. I haven't decided yet the kind of approach he needs."

"Just be yourself. I doubt whether you could be anything else, anyway. Acting a part wouldn't come easily to you, I guess. You'll win him over, just as you are. What do you think of him?"

"I haven't got behind the pallisade yet. I think it may be more difficult to break than you think. After all, put yourself in his place. If I've got it right, he lost both parents and grandparents in an air-crash when he was four. His world destroyed. Given a home by your grandparents, a solitary boy, falling by mischance into the hands of a sadistic nanny. Then he lost your grandfather, to whom he had become deeply attached, when he was only nine. Now he's faced with another home in a strange country where they don't even speak his language. Putting myself in his shoes, I should think the world a frightening, cruel place, and it would take a lot to reassure me."

"I agree. But youth is resilient. And Philippe's not a weak boy. The sooner we get him back and embarked on this new life instead of leaving him a prey to his fears about it, the better."

"Your grandmother wants to see how Philippe and I get along first. And whether I fit the bill."

"You will."

"Didn't we agree that reality should not break into this evening, though?"

"We did. Difficult to keep it out. Here, finish up this champagne with me. That will help to keep reality at bay."

"Well, since a romantic legend is not out of place, perhaps, don't you think it's touching that your grandfather never really got over his youthful love affair with my grandmother?"

"Not so touching for my grandmother, perhaps," said Pierre drily. "How did you know about that?"

"Janet told me. She wanted to prepare me for a possibly chilly welcome from your grandmother. I didn't sense any hostility, though. Only a concentrated examination of the candidate, which I must confess I find a little unnerving."

"Whatever passions may have been aroused in the distant past, ever since I've known Grandmother she's been the same shrewd, sceptical, detached observer of the human scene, singularly devoid of emotion of any sort. A strict believer in duty. Not exactly a cosy woman to live with."

"Partly the result of knowing that she didn't come first with her husband, perhaps. She'd be bound to know, without anything being spoken. And it's not a happy experience, being an also-ran."

He eyed her thoughtfully, and something in his expression made her add hurriedly, "That is, if it isn't just a legend. Hard to imagine that the old people you know were ever young, somehow."

"No legend. Not to my grandfather, anyway. He left a package for Mirabel Rainwood when he died. Gave it to me the last time I saw him. Asked me to be sure she got it. From the look of it, I'd say it contained letters."

"Devotion of a life-time. And with little to sustain it. The English channel between them, and few contacts, I'm sure. Grandma would never have strayed an inch."

"Perhaps that's why it lasted. A dream unspoiled by reality. That's what my grandmother would say, I've no doubt."

"And you? Do you believe real love wouldn't last all that time?"

"I think one could be haunted by a sense of loss all one's life. But time has a way of cooling everything off. I shouldn't get too misty-eyed over it."

"Not misty-eyed. Just a bit muzzy. Too much champagne."

"Ah, you see I'm playing the part in the true romantic tradition of lovely innocent girl, plied with too much champagne, carried off to dizzy seduction, to awaken next morning in a state of shock and with a blinding headache."

"You haven't got the right props. Where's the top hat, scarlet lined cloak and silver-topped, ebony swordstick?"

"With the gardenia in the cloak-room," he replied gravely.

"Sir, you would answer to my brother for your dastardly conduct."

"You don't need a brother," said Pierre, laughing. "The recollection of Mirabel Rainwood's eyes would be far more effective than a sword. I've never known anyone who can make you feel more like a prisoner at the bar than your grandmother, yet her courtesy is unswerving. I saw her briefly just before we came here. She told me to take care

of you, adding that you were very inexperienced in worldly
ways and far too trusting."

"Never! Did she really? Well, I suppose we never grow
up in old people's eyes."

"She wasn't so far out at that," he said, standing up and
holding out his hands. "Come on. 'Tales from the Vienna
Woods.' We're getting near the end."

Dancing with him, she felt happy and half in love with
him. He was utterly delightful that evening. Who would
have thought he would so enter into the spirit of it? Must
be the Gallic half of him. No Englishman that she knew
would have done so. Far too stiff and afraid of feeling a
fool.

While the 'Tritsch Tratsch Polka' was played, they
clapped to the rhythm with the other onlookers, and finally
swung round the dance floor again to the last waltz, inevitably the 'Blue Danube'.

Glad of the cool night air in the park afterwards,
Antonia sang the 'Blue Danube' as they lingered by the
floodlit fountain.

"You sound happy," observed Pierre.

"I am. Thank you for a lovely evening."

"I enjoyed it, too. Quite out of the blue. I never expected
to be taking part in such festivities. Years since I did anything like this. I was anticipating a very sober visit, un-
tangling my grandfather's affairs in a house of mourning.
Not that Grandfather would disapprove of this evening.
The reverse. He had a lively spirit."

"And yet you brought a dinner jacket with you."

"Because I have to go to Paris for a few days to see my
grandfather's solicitor, and he has invited me to share a box
at the opera with him and his wife one evening."

"Well, I'm sorry I didn't have a long, romantic dress
for the occasion. Not that I'm exactly the type."

"Who wants to be a type?"

"My cousin, Susan. She's the type. She would look absolutely irresistible in those off-the-shoulder nineteenth century ball dresses. You remember her? She was next to you at Grandma's tea-party."

"Ah yes. A very delectable meringue. You have a better figure for that style of dress, though. Susan's rather short for it. A pale honey colour, your ball dress should be. Lovely with your colouring. Hair up. Long diamond drop ear-rings."

"And an emerald green velvet cloak to go with your black and scarlet one. I could never run to diamond ear-rings, though. They'd have to be diamanté."

"What about your rich protector? But I forgot. Not in the Rainwood tradition. Well, never mind. Diamanté would sparkle almost as well. I can't cap your evening with a horse-drawn carriage all the way home, but I think we can get one to the station, and pick up a prosaic taxi there. There's even a full moon. Just everything is laid on tonight."

"Now nice of you to indulge my fantasy so, Pierre!"

And they were driven along the main thoroughfare of the town in an open horse-drawn carriage behind the stocky figure of a cockaded coachman.

"It seems more like Austria than Switzerland," observed Antonia, enjoying the clip-clop of the horses.

"Its geographic situation makes the German influence strong in this part of Switzerland. I don't know whether you've noticed yet, but German is the language most often spoken, with French and English the runners-up."

"I like it here. Gay and friendly."

"Well, it's a tourist country that sets out to be just that. Allow me," he added, handing her out of the carriage with a flourish.

In the taxi, driving through the woods, she was aware at last of tiredness creeping over her after the experiences of that long day. Already, it seemed an age since they had arrived at Heathrow in the chill of that early hour of the morning. Pierre put his arm round her and she rested her head on his shoulder, drowsy, happy and at ease with him. Perhaps that was the most surprising aspect of this surprising evening. She had found him so disconcerting before. Now, after one short evening of pleasure, she felt so comfortable with him. Perhaps in the morning, it would all be different. Perhaps the music and the champagne and the whole glamorous escapist atmosphere had bewitched her.

In the hall of the chalet, blinking a little in the light, she thanked him again for the evening.

"I'll never forget it," she said, smiling at him. "An enchanted evening. It was kind of you to play up to it."

"My pleasure. Good night, Tonie."

He kissed her, then, gently, without haste. Then said, with a crooked little smile.

"Off to bed with you before I forget Mirabel Rainwood's searching eyes."

She turned at the top of the stairs. He was lighting a cigarette, his back turned to her. Then he went out of the front door again.

In her room, the moon made artificial light unnecessary as she crossed to the window and looked out. Pierre was walking slowly along the gravelled path, and came to a halt by the low boundary wall, gazing across the lake towards the mountains beyond, cold and pale in the moonlight. She could see the glowing end of his cigarette. She drew the curtains together, still half entranced by the evening, wishing that he had not remembered Mirabel Rainwood's eyes quite so readily.

When, ready for bed, she drew the curtains back again and opened the window, he was still there, sitting on the wall, looking remote, absorbed, lost in a world of his own. A stranger again.

5

Revelations in an Alpine Meadow

BY THE END of the first week at the chalet, Antonia was able to mark up only very small gains in winning Philippe's confidence. He was unnaturally polite and obedient, but slipped away on his own whenever he could, and revealed little of his feelings. She had brought one of E. Nesbit's books and a science fiction adventure story to read with him, considering this the most painless method of improving his knowledge of English. He showed little interest in science fiction, but seemed to enjoy *The Treasure Seekers*, and they made good progress with it. But talking to him, trying to draw him out on the subject of his hobbies, his likes and dislikes, she made little progress. His lack of vitality worried her, too, although that could be attributed to his recent illness. She spent a good part of each day with him, but took care to keep the atmosphere casual and free of restraint, and by the end of the week he was at least able to take the initiative now and again and address some remarks to her instead of merely giving brief polite replies to her questions and observations.

She expressed guarded optimism to Pierre as they walked down to the village one evening.

"At least I'm pretty sure that he's no longer afraid of me," she said.

"It would be an odd child who'd be afraid of you, Tonie."

"But it's not easy to know what is going on in his mind. Fear of the unknown future, perhaps."

"You're going to bridge that for him, I'm sure. I shouldn't worry overmuch about his reserve. It's a sign of strength, in a way. He battles it out inside. Philippe's no weakling. He comes of good stock. He'll unburden himself in his own time. And don't forget, there's the language difficulty. How do you rate his English?"

"Not bad. He's very intelligent and is trying. If all goes according to plan, I think he could be ready for his English school by the autumn and not be handicapped by language difficulties."

"You're willing to tackle the job, then?"

"I want to, very much. That boy's a challenge. I like what I know of him so far, and I want to help him. I hope I can. But it rests with your grandmother."

"You've made a good impression, and I may add that my grandmother is hard to please and never lavish with her praises. The point is, she's contrasting you now with Janet, much to the latter's disadvantage, and wishing that Paul had married someone like you. She does not approve of careers for married women. They should choose one or the other, she maintains."

"A bit hard, if you love your work and love your man. Very Victorian."

"Oh, my grandmother's no prude. It's just that she's strong for family life, and thinks that marriage means children, and that the whole set-up requires the full-time attentions of the wife if it's to succeed. I don't think she would be shocked at looser arrangements outside of marriage."

"Do you agree with her?"

"How can I in theory if I didn't in practice? I married a girl with a brilliant career. We never contemplated a

family. Both my brother and I are sore disappointments
to my grandmother in that respect."

"I'm sorry," said Antonia, startled and confused. "I
didn't know you were married. Grandma didn't say ...
We didn't discuss ..."

"No reason why you should. My wife died three years
ago. But what about your views? You indicated pretty
firmly that you were unlikely to marry. A foolish pro-
nouncement, my grandmother said. A surprising one, I
thought. Any special reason? Want to keep your freedom?"

"Well, you could say that."

"I doubt whether you'll be allowed to, you know. There
must have been attempts on it before."

She was silent, and he glanced at her quickly. Then said,
"Forgive me. Some things are not for discussion. At a guess,
the attempts didn't come from the right quarter. Correct?"

"You're very shrewd."

"Not really. I've some experience of lost love myself. I
can pick up the scent of it. But at your age, Tonie, it can't
be final."

"Second best?"

"Oh, I'm all for compromise. Where would we be without it? This is a pleasant spot. Shall we share a pot of
coffee?"

The terrace of the restaurant overlooked the lake, close
to the landing stage from which one of the white pleasure
steamers was just pulling away. The evening was fine and
warm and they sat at a table by the balustrade, which was
adorned by long boxes of geraniums. In the mellow light
of the evening sun, the lake took on a burnished appearance, and the wooded slopes that came down to the water
and the mountains beyond were all brushed with the golden
serenity of the evening.

She pulled her eyes back to Pierre's dark, intelligent face
opposite her. She had not thought of Darrel during this
week in Switzerland until Pierre's words had brought back

the old ache. But it wasn't quite such an empty ache, she
felt. The future had a purpose and a challenge once more,
and the present was absorbing. And, for the first time since
that holiday in Ireland, she had met a man who made her
deeply aware of her sex. Other men she had liked on a
casual, friendly basis, always conscious that Darrel's hold
on her was too strong to give them anything but a pale
significance beside him. But Pierre Valais had made his own
deep mark on her. She found him attractive, puzzling,
maddening and utterly charming. And she knew that this
week in Switzerland together had aroused his interest in
her. Not much, perhaps. But it was there. During their
first encounters, he had just been jockeying her into accepting this job of looking after Philippe, knowing that it would
not be easy to find anyone, impatient at being saddled with
the task, rather bored with her but anxious not to put her
off.

Now, as she met his dark eyes, she knew that the situation
between them had changed. He still saw her as a child, but
one he was now interested in, willing to indulge, and whose
enjoyment of these new surroundings he was happy to
share.

"Those Alpine flowers," she said, a little confused by
the expression on his face. "Any special places you'd
recommend?"

"You must have read my thoughts. I was about to suggest
a day out tomorrow. We could take a train from Lakendorf,
get out at one of the stations up the valley and walk up
through the meadows to the next station. The train stops
at all the little villages up the valley, and footpaths through
the meadows are plentiful and good. My grandmother is
taking Philippe into Lakendorf tomorrow to kit him out
with clothes. An opportunity for you to have a day off.
Does it appeal?"

"Very much. And having shown me the ropes, I can take
Philippe for a picnic there next week, perhaps."

"Yes. He likes going on trains."

"So do I."

"The eternal child," he said, smiling. "Wish I hadn't to go to Paris on Monday. These legal tangles are tiresome."

"But you'll have the opera."

"So I shall. Like music?"

"Very limited knowledge of it. But I realise that I'm missing a lot. I enjoy the obvious choices. Beethoven, Chopin, Schubert. But I only paddle occasionally at the fringe. Through radio. I've never been to a concert."

"Sad," he said, shaking his head.

"I know. But my jobs have always taken me to outlandish places. By choice, of course. I like the country and an outdoor life. Never could abide cities."

"Well, happily, records and broadcasting make it possible to enjoy the best of all worlds."

"What a lovely colourful landscape this is!" exclaimed Antonia, as her eyes shifted from the geraniums, blazing in the light of the sinking sun, across the blue lake to the green wooded slopes on the far side up which the red cabin of a ski-lift was slowly climbing towards the high mountain slopes.

"Just what I was thinking," said Pierre lazily, but his eyes were on her hair, red-gold in the sunshine.

"Hope it's like this tomorrow," she said, still following the progress of the red cabin.

* * *

The little train wended its way up the valley at a modest speed and had wide windows from which Antonia could enjoy the passing countryside. Pierre, she found, had not exaggerated the beauty of the Alpine meadows, for they resembled a rich tapestry of pink, blue, white and gold as the train ran through them, following the course of a twisting river.

When they had left the train, their footpath, too, followed

the course of the river for some time, then led across a meadow cutting off a loop in the river, and she was able to examine the wide variety of flowers at close range. She recognised only a few, the gold vetches and daisies, some orchids, campion and scabious. Growing to a foot or more in height, moving gently in the breeze, the flowers and grasses absorbed her, and her companion sat down on a bank and lit a cigarette while she lingered among them.

"I need my botanist friend here," she observed. "He would know them all."

"Why bother with names? They are just as lovely nameless."

"That's an unscientific attitude that would pain him, but I agree. An interesting subject to study, though."

"Is your botanist friend a professional, then, or just a keen amateur?"

"A professional. He's director of a Horticultural Station in Sussex. I'd have liked to work there, but I had no qualifications." She looked up from the flowers to find him studying her with a thoughtful expression which made her add hurriedly, "The only meadows to compare with these are those I saw in Ireland."

"Ah, that's a country I don't know. An unhappy one."

"But so beautiful."

She found herself telling him about it as they walked on. The wonderful summer she had spent there, when the sun shone for most of the time, and which, in retrospect, seemed like a golden dream. Pierre said little, encouraging her with a word or two now and again.

"You say 'We'. Who were your companions in this Paradise?" he asked.

"My cousin, Nick, and my friends, Darrel and Jean. They weren't married then. We met them there. Nick was staying at the same hotel as they were. I was staying with my uncle and aunt, nearby."

"It has a special significance for you, that holiday, I think."

"Just one of those rare magic times when everything is right. Stardust. Since then, no stardust. Except one Viennese night," she added lightly, realising that she was revealing more than she intended to this skilled manipulator.

"Well, we must see if we can conjure up some more stardust for you, and then I can bask in its reflected light. Your friend, Darrel. Would he be the botanical expert?"

"Yes. Dr. Darrel Brynton. Don't those crickets sound jolly? The right accompaniment to a hot summer day. You know, I can't bear the thought that all this lovely assembly will soon be cut for hay."

"The cows will appreciate it. And that reminds me that I'm peckish. If I remember rightly, they do superb omelettes at the little inn at the next village. Suit you?"

"Nothing better."

They had come out beside the river again, and the cool sound of fast running water accompanied them for the rest of the way to the village.

The inn faced the village square, quiet in the noonday heat, and they had their meal on a tree-shaded table outside. The omelettes, brought to them by a smiling, buxom girl, were as good as Pierre had predicted, and they lingered over a jug of coffee afterwards. Their energy diminished by this intake, they sauntered slowly along the twisting riverside path that afternoon towards the next village station, halting for a rest on the bank half way.

"How long will you be in Paris?" she asked.

"Three or four days. Depends how things go. I had intended to stay the week, but I'm finding life more attractive here than I expected. You've made me enjoy myself, Tonie. Do you know that? Made me feel young and carefree. I'd forgotten what it was like."

"I've done nothing. Only enjoyed myself, thanks to you and this lovely place."

"You don't have to do anything. Your enthusiasm, your vitality, is enough. It's like your hair. It reflects light. I feel we've come quite a long way this week, don't you?"

"Yes, after a not very promising start."

He laughed and took her hand.

"I'm a morose devil sometimes. Forgive me."

"You're rather a puzzle. You give so little of yourself away, although you're very clever at winkling information out of me. Already I've told you pretty well all my life story."

"Not quite."

"I haven't your finesse, so I can only ask direct questions if I want to know you better."

"And do you?" He was lying on his back and his black eyes danced up at her as she sat looking down at him.

"Yes, I do. How long have you worked with your friend on the fruit farm?"

"Oh, about a year."

"Do you like the work? Somehow, you don't strike me as a farmer."

"I'm not. I see to the administrative and financial side. Kevin, who knows all about growing fruit, but not much about finance, had got himself in a right old financial mess. I know little about farming, though I'm learning a bit, but I'm not bad at organising. Hence, the partnership. My part is only a minor one."

"Is that what you wanted to do?"

"I offered to do it because Kevin is an old friend, and because I wanted to find a quiet country retreat where I could work on the translation of a French opera into English, and on articles for a music magazine."

"Music. That's your thing, then."

"You could put it like that."

His sceptical tone stopped her interrogation, and she said haltingly,

"I'm sorry, Pierre. I don't want to seem inquisitive. Forget it. Not my business."

"Mine is a sorry, unsatisfactory history, my dear. Profitless to discuss."

"I know how you feel. I felt just the same at the family tea-party when I knew they were all going to ask me what I'd been doing, curious about what sort of a hash I'd made of yet another brief job that had promised well. It's disheartening, having to talk about failures and disappointments. You'd rather forget them. Put them behind you."

"Have you had so many, then?"

"Well," she said frankly, "you could really call my life a bit of a mess so far. Several promising starts, leading to dead ends."

"Tell me."

"I've never had a very clear idea of what I wanted to do by way of earning my living, so I took my mother's advice and embarked on secretarial training. I hated it. Being indoors. Especially after that summer in Ireland. So I threw it up. Tried to get into Darrel's Horticultural Station, but he wouldn't have me. Not without any qualifications. Then I went to Canada for a year, staying at the ranch of a friend, where they bred and trained horses. I liked the work, but got homesick. Came home and took a job teaching the daughter of a millionaire to ride. She was partially crippled after an accident. I was led to believe that it might lead to our running a riding school, financed by her grandfather, but that fell through and I was told my services were no longer required. Then I went up north to help in a privately run nature reserve. But the finances ran out there. So I was back home again. Not exactly a brilliant record," she concluded with a lightness which did not deceive him.

"Anybody with your temperament is bound to be disillusioned. You expect too much. But your present assignment will be a resounding success, I predict."

"It must be," she said, with a fervour that surprised him.

"And the unrequited love affair? Have you got over it?"

"It haunts me. Not so much lately, though. Other things to occupy me."

"How long has it lasted?"

"Three years."

"You're very constant. Especially if, as I imagine, you have little contact to sustain it. No hope?"

"Never was. He's happily married. Sees me only as a child."

"And yet you can't cut clear. Foolish, Tonie. You're too young to live with a dream. But I don't doubt someone will obliterate it for you one day. Romantic dreams are all very well, but they leave the flesh hungry and frustrated."

She was silent for a while, then said abruptly,

"Were you happy, Pierre? In your marriage, I mean."

"Very."

"Then, in a way, we're both haunted. For you, of course, so much worse. You achieved happiness, and lost it. I never had any hope of achieving it."

"We could console each other, you mean?"

"Well, you said you've enjoyed yourself more this week than for years. And so have I."

"Quite right. We will continue the medicine. Live in the present and stop looking back. But if we don't move now, we're going to miss the train."

He pulled her to her feet, and kissed her gently.

"Nice medicine," he said, smiling.

As they stepped out along the path more briskly, she thought that he, too, like Darrel, could only see her as a child.

6

The Empty Spaces

ON THE FOLLOWING Monday, after Pierre had left for Paris, Antonia marked up her first real gain with Philippe. After reading with him in the garden most of the morning, he went off on an errand to the village after lunch. When he did not return for tea, she went to look for him.

It took about twenty minutes to walk down to the lakeside village, and she expected to find him on the promenade watching the steamers come and go, a favourite occupation, but he was nowhere to be seen. Enquiry at the little café which sold ice creams and soft drinks elicited the information that he had been in and bought an ice cream, and then had been seen going off in the direction of the church up the hill.

Walking up the hill, she was relieved to see him ahead of her coming out of the gate of the churchyard, where the well-tended little flowery plots made it resemble a garden. He did not see her, and turned and walked up the path with a dragging step and lowered head. In his tight blue jeans and skimpy blue and white cotton jersey, he looked as thin as a tadpole, and there was a desolate, lonely air about him that went to her heart. She called him, but he seemed not to hear.

"Hullo, Phil. We were wondering where you'd got to," she said as she caught up with him. When he turned, she saw that tears had left dirty trails down his cheeks, and the front of his jersey had a long green stain down it. He said nothing. She had the impression that he was too miserable to speak.

"Did you post the letter and get the stamps, Phil?" she asked gently.

He nodded, dug into his jeans and handed her a crumpled collection of stamps.

"Good boy," she said, putting a hand on his shoulder for a moment, judging it best to say no more until he had collected himself.

The sun was hot as they plodded uphill, and when they came to the welcome shade of a strip of woodland, Philippe said in his careful English, "My grandfather saved Grandfather Valais's life when they were in the Resistance."

"Did he? You must be very proud of him."

"Yes. They had lots of adventures. They blew up trains."

"You must tell me all about it some time. Perhaps tomorrow. I thought we'd go on a train up the valley and have a picnic. You could fish in the river. And tell me about the Resistance."

He nodded, and sniffed. Just before they reached the chalet, a squirrel ran across their path and they scrambled down after it until it darted up a tree and disappeared. Philippe climbed back ahead of her up the slope, as agile as a monkey, and when he had regained the path, he watched her and held out his hand with a shy smile as she approached. She took it, and allowed him to use his limited strength to pull her back on to the path. She smiled down at him and moved her fingers in his unruly black hair.

"Thanks, Phil," she said.

No more was spoken between them. He darted away to clean up for tea, and Antonia lingered a moment by the low wall looking over the lake, conscious of an achievement. For the first time, they had made some sort of contact, and she felt as pleased as though she had just climbed the peak of the mountain she was looking at.

She consolidated her gain the next day, when Philippe obviously enjoyed the train journey, and proved a keen but unsuccessful fisherman. His enjoyment of this simple outing made it plain to her that his life had been greatly circumscribed by the age of his guardians, for Madame Valais seldom ventured far on foot, and old age and failing health had doubtless made it impossible for Louis Valais to take the boy around. Madame Valais was quite right in wanting younger guardians for Philippe.

But if Louis Valais had been physically limited, he had obviously been very close to the boy and had talked a lot to him about the past, for she was regaled at intervals throughout that day with hair-raising tales of the exploits of the Resistance movement in the last war, in all of which Philippe's grandfather emerged as a hero. Louis Valais, Antonia thought, must have been a very kind and understanding person.

That evening, after dinner, she was able to give an optimistic report to Madame Valais.

"I really feel we're on a hopeful footing now. He trusts me, I think. I've been talking to him a little about his new home in England. Trying to allay his fears. I think I succeeded, up to a point. Belmont Hall is in a lovely situation. Open country all around and a river on one boundary. A good environment for a boy."

"Good. Good. I'm very pleased with you, Antonia. I only wish you were going to be a permanent fixture in Philippe's life."

"Well, I shall try not to disappear out of it when he goes to school, but I have to earn my living."

"Yes. A pity Janet is not more like you. But she will doubtless do her best. You and Pierre. You've taken a liking to each other, I fancy. Haven't seen him in such good spirits for years. Not since his wife died."

"It was a happy marriage, I believe."

"Yes. They were passionately in love with each other. One of those rare marriages, made in heaven."

"What sort of person was she?"

"Claire? Lovely, gifted. Like many who die young, she had more to give the world than most. She was already making a name for herself in opera when she died. But she was never, I fancy, strong enough for such a taxing profession. Pierre brought her here once or twice for a rest."

"It was music that drew them together, I suppose."

"Yes. Pierre taught at the college of music. He met her there. Afterwards, he gave up teaching to accompany Claire at recitals and manage her career for her. She relied on him completely. Had little confidence in herself, in spite of her great gift. He gave her confidence, spared her the organising problems, made all the travelling arrangements. They were wrapped up in music and in each other. A tragedy."

"How long had they been married when she died?"

"Nearly four years. Some spinal infection she picked up abroad, the doctors said. She was ill for only a few weeks. And it changed Pierre out of all recognition. At first, he seemed to have turned to stone, and then to a mocking parody of himself. You've been good for him. He's been more natural here this past week. I've not seen a great deal of him since Claire's death, and each time I found him a stranger. Now, I think a thaw has set in."

"He didn't go back to teaching music?"

"No. Cut away from the musical world they'd known completely. But went on studying, writing about it. I think he wanted to avoid people who had known Claire, and, of course, she was well known. She had a great future in front of her. But God disposes. Now, Pierre should put it behind him. Marry again. A girl like you would be good for him. A home and family. A settled life."

"He probably doesn't want to settle for second best."

The old woman looked at Antonia with a sceptical pursing of her lips, then said drily, "He's not such a fool. Who doesn't settle for second best in this life? Lucky if it's not far lower down the list than that. Only ignorant young people think in terms of perfection. Romantic notions. Pierre isn't different from most men in liking his comforts. And he's a realist."

"An unhappy marriage is no comfort."

"He would have to choose sensibly, of course, but Pierre is no fool. You find him attractive? Yes?"

"Yes."

"And he shows liking for you. I should be pleased if you married him, Antonia. It would be a good, sensible match."

"You have only known me a week, Madame," said Antonia, smiling. "Are matches made so precipitately in France?"

"You come of good stock, and are not difficult to know, my dear. Unlike most young people these days, you do not hide yourself."

"Pierre has no such thought, I assure you. I could never hold a candle to Claire."

"You don't have to. He wants no reminders. A stable home. A woman in his life again. Children. You would fit the bill admirably."

Antonia, finding this mundane attitude to marriage somewhat indigestible, and by no means enamoured of the earthy and useful role being allotted to her, said firmly, "Marriages of convenience don't appeal to me and end up unsatisfactorily, I'm sure. Particularly for Pierre, who knew such happiness before."

"*Ma foi!* Such romantic nonsense! Pierre and Claire had a few passionate, exciting years. Yes. But do you think the future would have stayed like that? Claire would have become, there is little doubt, a world-famous soprano, travelling the world from opera house to opera house. And

Pierre? Following her star all his life. Doing the organising chores while she was fêted. He, like most men, is an egoist. He has talent of his own, but she would have had the lime-light. His life would necessarily have been subservient to her career. And he is a passionate man underneath what you see as a cool surface now. And that means a possessive man. Would he have been happy all his life sharing his wife with the world? Perhaps getting the smallest share, too. I am telling you, and I am an old woman with a lot of experience of life, that the romantic idyll of Pierre's short marriage would undoubtedly have turned into something less idyllic over the years. Men are not made in the mould of self-sacrifice."

This was the abrasive Madame Valais of Janet's warning, and Antonia wondered if the old lady's poor opinion of men and her scorn of romance owed anything to her husband's romantic attachment to Mirabel Rainwood.

"And what," asked Antonia gravely but with a twinkle in her eyes, "does the woman gain in this second-best marriage of convenience?"

"From Pierre? An intelligent companion, a strong sup-port, a good lover. He would discharge his obligations to his marriage honourably, I am sure."

"No hazards? No hidden vices?"

"He's no more unselfish than most men. Strong-willed, to be sure, and with a fiery temper which he keeps pretty well controlled but is there, all the same. Intolerant, too. Much room for improvement, and needs careful handling. But I've known worse. He also has a rather impudent sense of humour, which I see you have, too, Miss. But think over my words. You could, if you put your mind to it, marry my grandson."

"The decision would not be his?"

A sceptical little smile flickered over the sallow, lined face of the old lady as she got stiffly to her feet.

"A determined woman is more than a match for any man," she observed.

* * *

Antonia filled the days of Pierre's absence by consolidating her gains with Philippe while they went on steamer trips round the lake and long, leisurely walks through the meadows and lower wooded slopes of the mountains. As his confidence with her increased, she found him a delightful companion. Not very talkative even in his own language, and never boisterous, he nevertheless displayed an alert interest in his surroundings and in her knowledge of countryside matters, and never seemed bored. She talked a lot about Belmont Hall, hoping to dispel his fears and build a bridge between his two lives.

"Can we fish in the river there?" he asked.

"Yes."

"And go for walks on our own, like this?"

"Of course. We shall also have to do some lessons. Especially English. And your arithmetic isn't good, I'm told."

He pulled a face and looked up at her from under his long, dark lashes.

"I. is bad. I don't like it."

"I never did, either."

"Then perhaps you can't teach me."

"Enough. If not, I have a very clever brother. He might help us."

This did not meet with any great enthusiasm, and he ran on ahead towards the waterfall which was the object of their walk that afternoon. He was tiring less easily now than in their first week, she thought. Their conversation had given her an idea, though. He was unusually backward in arithmetic, she had learned. Jonathan might well be willing to give some time in the summer vacation to coaching

Philippe. It would be good practice for the teaching profession he had already chosen for his career.

Pierre was due back that evening, and she was looking forward to his return with an eagerness that surprised her. He had only been away four days, but she had missed him.

It was when she went into Pierre's bedroom that afternoon to water the geraniums in the window box that she noticed among a jumble of papers the music magazine he had been reading in the train. Inside, she found what had caused that terrible expression of pain on his face. An article on Claire Valais, the distinguished young soprano, whose early death had been such a loss to the world of music. It gave details of her career, her successes in opera houses all over the world, and referred briefly to her talented husband and his part in her career, finishing up with a list of her opera recordings. Antonia wished there had been a photograph, but the article gave a sufficiently graphic description of this lovely, talented young singer to make the extent of Pierre's loss plain to her. As she put the magazine back, she was conscious of a passionate longing to console him and a realisation that such consolation could only ever be partial. But, thinking of his happy mood on that first champagne evening, and his warm, cheerful friendliness since, she felt encouraged by the progress so far made.

It was evident at dinner that evening, however, that his mood had changed whilst he was away. He looked tired, and the light-hearted front he put on seemed brittle, and an effort. The business affairs had apparently been sorted out satisfactorily, however, and Antonia could only suppose that the social side of his visit had not been wildly successful. Or, perhaps, too successful, and this was a hangover.

"Come for a walk, Tonie," he said abruptly, after his grandmother had finished her lengthy questioning about the legal problems and had gone to bed. "I need some air."

It was growing dark as they walked down to the lake and took the footpath beside it which led to Lakendorf.

"Did you enjoy your visit to Paris?" she asked.

"Parts of it were all right," he said, non-committally.

"The opera?"

"Very good performance."

"What was it?"

"*The Masked Ball.*"

"Reminds me of our Viennese evening."

"Not quite so light-hearted as that. Tell me what you've been up to."

She told him about her excursions with Philippe and her idea about some coaching from Jonathan.

"It would be a pity for Philippe to start with any additional handicap, and Jonathan would be quite happy to oblige, I'm sure. He's a born teacher. In his first year at Cambridge."

"Sounds a good idea. Philippe's in luck. Overdue for it, too. You'd better take me on some excursions, and infect me with your wide-eyed enthusiasm, too."

"Would you be mocking?"

"Far from it. I mean it. You have a most beneficial influence on my spirits, Tonie. When everything seems sour and flat, you inject some sparkle."

"Like soda water, you mean."

He laughed and took her arm.

"Something like."

The moon was rising over the wooded slopes on the far side of the lake, and the lights shone out from the scattered villages like brooches pinned on the dark cloak of the woods. The water lapped gently beside them. A swan drifted by, pale and ghostly, and disappeared behind an overhanging tree.

They walked on in silence. Intuitively, Antonia knew that Pierre was haunted that night. The ghost of his wife, brought back by the opera, perhaps. Or by friends who had known her. She sensed his pain, and wanted to ease it.

"Feel like walking as far as Lakendorf?" he asked suddenly. "We can have a drink and some music in the Kursaal. Always bright lights and music there. We can get a taxi back."

"Good idea," she said, thinking that if he wanted it that way, she would play along with him.

His mood was a strange one of restless edginess that night. There was a concert of light music in the Kursaal, and he ordered drinks at a table near the orchestra, but tired of this after half an hour and took her to see the gaming room and then the picture gallery, finishing up outside in the gardens where there was a fireworks display to mark some anniversary.

"It's a popular pastime in the tourist season. Always some special occasion that can be given as a reason for fireworks."

"They're fun," said Antonia, watching a shower of green and gold stars burst in the sky and drift down. "I remember when I was a kid, my great-aunt Lucille gave a wonderful fireworks party in the garden of her country home. A fabulous affair. All the Rainwood clan there. And the biggest bonfire I've ever seen. I've never forgotten it."

"Lucille? I don't think I remember her name."

"Grandma Rainwood's sister. She ran a chain of beauty salons. Very successful. Went to live in Geneva, and died there about a year ago. Left a packet of money to her young male secretary and not a penny to the family. *That* was a talking point at the family gatherings, I can tell you."

"A break-away from the Rainwood tradition."

"Yes. We didn't see much of her. She travelled a lot. I only remember being fascinated by her blue hair. I thought it such an odd colour. She was always heavily made up and loaded with jewels. I regarded her with some awe. But it was a splendid fireworks party."

She knew that he was only half listening, and fell silent. How long ago it seemed, that party. How little she had achieved since. Her life had been rather like these rockets, she thought. Zooming off in various directions, only to have the bright stars of her expectations falling and dwindling into nothingness.

She started as she felt Pierre's arm round her shoulders.

"You look pensive, and I'm poor company. You and I indulge far too much in looking back. And wasting present opportunities," he concluded with a brittle edge to his voice.

He led her away from the crowds and the fireworks along a dark walk between thick belts of shrubs. When he stopped and took her in his arms, she yielded to his rough urgency, wanting to comfort him, help him to forget the tormenting mind and the memories, and finally catching some of that urgency in her own response. She had frustrations and memories to blot out, too. When at last he released her, she was trembling. She leaned against him for a few moments, saying nothing, feeling the wild beating of her heart, while he moved his hand gently over her hair. Then he said abruptly, "I didn't mean to wake the tiger. Let's go."

They went back through the gardens and along the brightly lit main thoroughfare of the town to the station, both silent. In the taxi, too, they said little. Pierre seemed wrapped in thought, and Antonia felt too shaken and confused to trust to speech.

Walking up the drive to the chalet, he took her arm and drew her down the flagged path that led to the front boundary wall.

"I'm sorry, Tonie. I shouldn't have taken you with me this evening. A bad mood. I was using you. I . . ."

"No need to explain. I know. I was willing to be used. I wanted to help you."

"Not used. That's too ugly and not accurate. I needed you."

"A little, yes. We said console each other. Remember?"

"I don't want you to get hurt."

"I get the consolation, too. It's two-way."

"Yes. But you're young. Innocent."

"Not too young to know about the pain of loss."

"No. That has surprised me. Your understanding. You're so lively, so full of enthusiasm. And yet you understand about loss. The empty spaces inside."

"I don't know that it's a question of age. Philippe knows about the empty spaces, I'm sure."

"Back home, this summer. We might build on it. What is between us."

"Yes."

"Not too deeply involved, Tonie. I never want that again. You must understand, and not get hurt."

"Friends. For consolation."

"Sounds very neat, but you, my dear, are not a girl to do anything by halves, I fancy."

"Are you?"

"Part of me has calcified. Just not alive any more. A poor bargain, really."

"Not to worry. I understand," she said lightly.

"Then, that accepted, I think it could be a good pact between us."

"So do I. Do you know that poem of Emily Brontë's called *Remembrance*?"

"No. Tell me."

"I can only remember a bit.

But, when the days of golden dreams had perished,
And even Despair was powerless to destroy;
Then did I learn how existence could be cherished,
Strengthened, and fed, without the aid of joy.

The whole poem wings home, but those four lines have stayed with me. Worth remembering, I think."

"Yes, indeed." He put a hand on her shoulder. "Thank you for wanting to help. A warm heart. For Philippe, as well. Our luck. We've only a few more days here. We must make the most of them."

But their few days stretched to a further week, for Paul telephoned the next evening to say that as Janet was going away on a week's refresher training course, he thought it might be a good idea if they postponed their return for a week, so that Janet could be there to welcome Philippe.

"A course!" exclaimed Madame Valais scornfully. "Are the techniques of physiotherapy so complex, then? That is how it will be. Career first, before her husband and Philippe. I'm thankful that you and Antonia will be at hand to make up for her deficiencies."

"Don't worry. Philippe will be well looked after," said Pierre.

"And you have work to do, as well as Janet. But you must stay away another week so that she can go on a course. Nothing is so important as her career. I tell you, Pierre, I wish you were married and had a home for the boy. I would much sooner have entrusted him to you."

"I've a penchant for career girls myself," said Pierre wickedly.

The old lady shook her head, expostulating angrily in French, but Antonia was pleased at the prospect of another week in Switzerland with Pierre. She had recognised his warning and had accepted it, but in his arms on the night of his return from Paris she had experienced the force of passion for the first time in her life, and knew that she was already more deeply involved with Pierre Valais than he would have wished.

7

The Bend in the River

AFTER AN UNEASY and subdued start, Philippe began to settle well into his new life at Belmont Hall. He clung at first to Antonia, but Janet's good-natured, common-sense attitude to him soon reassured him, although he stood somewhat in awe of Paul.

As the fine weeks of that June slid by, Antonia, too, found herself settling happily into her new life. She established a regular routine of lessons with Philippe, spent a lot of time out of doors with him, and enjoyed Pierre's frequent appearances. She went home each weekend, and knitted into life at the lodge during the week without difficulty, having her own bed-sitting room at the top of the house to retreat to, although Janet seemed to welcome her company in the evenings, when Paul, as often as not, was still immersed in his duties.

"I sometimes think I married Belmont Hall, not a man," she said drily one evening.

"A good thing you have an absorbing career of your own," said Antonia.

"Yes. The Hall is a splendid heritage from the past, of course. Worth all Paul's devotion. I wish he'd unbend a bit with Phil, though."

"Oh, I don't know. A kind detachment isn't without its

value. An authority Phil can respect. Something firm at his back. He needs that."

"It's good to see him happy and without that frightened look in his eyes. You've done marvels with him. Where is he, by the way?"

"Fishing with Tom, a boy from the village."

"The one who goes to the prep school?"

"Yes. A bit of luck, that. He's already talked enough about it to make Phil quite happy about going there in September."

"He'd better work hard at his lessons, then. The interview we had with the headmaster last Saturday made it clear that Phil's got a good deal of ground to make up. Not lacking in intelligence, obviously, but his schooling has been interrupted a lot. I think your idea about calling in your brother for a few sessions is a good one. Think he'll be willing? For a fee, of course."

"I expect so. I'll sound him out."

"He'll probably have more exciting things to do during the vacation."

"Not Jonathan. Academic matters are all that count with him. I sometimes wonder if he's human at all. All intellect. No emotions. That's why he finds me such an odd person. All emotions and little intellect, according to him."

"He's younger than you?"

"Two years. We've never been on the same wave-length, I'm afraid, but we get along amicably enough. Jonathan would never quarrel, anyway."

And so on two afternoons of each week from mid-July until the end of August, the tall, lanky, bespectacled Jonathan appeared at Belmont Hall and took upon himself to investigate the academic contents of Phillippe's mind, and remedy the deficiencies with a calm and precise thoroughness not altogether appreciated by the victim. Such single-mindedness of purpose, however, was more than a match for any slackness, and Antonia, thus freed of her duties on these afternoons, hired a pony from some nearby stables and went riding, or, when the number of visitors to Belmont Hall strained the resources of the staff, gave a hand in the refreshment room behind the stable block.

Sometimes it seemed to her that she was living in a dream, her imagination caught up by the grandeur of her surroundings, the spirit of the eighteenth century evoked by the massive grey stone house sleeping on in the summer sunshine, the treasures of the past preserved within its walls, the pastoral landscape surrounding it, the Poets' Walk.

And as the buttercups and daisies in the meadow surrounding the lodge gave way to harebells and scabious and scarlet pimpernels, and the mountain ash berries on the tree near the porch turned a brilliant orange and were raided by starlings and blackbirds, her friendship with Pierre ripened, too.

On a hot afternoon in August, one which she never forgot, she strolled across the grounds to the river boundary and walked along the high bank for a short way until she came to a seat at a bend in the river. It was a favourite retreat when she wanted to be alone. A shady, solitary spot, where she often saw kingfishers flashing up or down the stream, and on rare occasions, if she kept very still, could watch one fishing from an overhanging branch not far from the seat.

She was glad of the shade from the overhanging trees. Below her, the shallow water moved slowly, except for odd eddies where stones caused little swirling rushes of water. She never tired of the changing light and pattern of the water, dark green and gold on that day of unclouded sunshine. Opposite, some old willow trees moved gently in the soft breeze. From the overhanging trees along the river bank, odd leaves drifted down to the water, there to be carried slowly along towards the sea. Fishes were rising to the midges, making circles where they broke the water's surface. A beautiful, peaceful timelessness ruled there.

She found herself wishing that time would stop just then. On this hot summer day at the bend of the river. Happy at her success with Philippe, at the affection between them. Happy at her growing love for Pierre, and warmed by his evident affection for her. If she could only stop time here, at this perfect moment. She feared change now. Welcome at one time, now she viewed it warily, knowing how it had robbed her so often before. She gazed at the reflections of the trees in the water, half hypnotised by the flickering pattern, the soft whisper of the willow trees, the gentle rustle of the water.

She jumped as two hands came down on her shoulders.

"I thought I might find you here. Shall I break the spell?"

She smiled up at Pierre's dark face.

"Come and weave me another."

"You look as cool as a lettuce. It's a roaster today. It says much for your brother's skill as a teacher that he's nailed Philippe's attention to maths under the beech tree in the meadow on a day like this. Both as absorbed as squirrels with nuts."

"And allowing me to sit here, dreaming."

"Nice dreams?"

"Not dreams, exactly. Just a suspended state of tranquillity. Merging with the river. The only conscious thought, wishing it could all stop here. Nothing change."

"Like the figures on the Grecian urn. The immutable law of change, I'm afraid, can never be side-stepped."

Antonia sighed as she watched another yellowing leaf drift slowly down to the water.

"That leaf tells me so. Autumn is on the door-step."

"You've been happy here, haven't you?"

"Very happy."

"Any plans? After Philippe goes to school, I mean."

"I want to be near here. I would have liked to join the staff, help look after this place, but of course the winter season means reduction of staff, and Paul won't have any vacancies until next spring. In any case I must move from the lodge. It's better for Paul and Janet to have their home to themselves. Third parties can be awkward."

"You haven't been, I'm sure."

"Paul and Janet. There's a bit of a strain there, I feel. It will be better resolved on their own."

"M'm. Could be. Nothing seriously wrong, is there?"

"I don't think so. Janet feels the strain of being pulled in several directions. Paul and Belmont Hall, her job, and now Phil. Nothing definite said. I just sense it."

"What are your plans, then?"

"No hurry. But I may take a job at the riding school where I hire a pony sometimes, and find lodgings in the village. The owner needs an assistant. I haven't thought about it seriously yet, though. I'm enjoying the present. Not wanting change."

"Well, I shall be moving out, too, in the autumn."

She could not hide her look of startled dismay as her eyes met his.

"You're going away?"

"Kevin's getting married in December. His wife won't want me occupying half the house. It was only a temporary arrangement anyway, while I sorted Kevin's affairs out and started a proper accounting system. And sorted myself out, too."

"You mean, you're giving up your work at the farm?"

"Not altogether. But a day a month would suffice for the accounts. I can concentrate now on being what some pedantic people term a musicologist."

"And that means doing what?"

"Journalism for music magazines. Record reviews. Scripts for broadcasting. And I've still got a good deal of work to do on translating that French opera libretto into English. I've had in mind for some time, too, a project on the lives of one or two neglected composers."

"Plenty of scope, then," she said, conscious that his words seemed to be taking him away from her, opening an enormous gap.

"Yes. Have to find a suitable base for work now."

"In London?" she asked, the glory of the day now utterly dimmed.

"No. I finished with London years ago. Somewhere round here, I hope."

"That's better," she said, the cloud lifting.

He took her hand and looked at it thoughtfully for a few moments, then said, "That consolation pact we made. For me, it's been enormously successful. For you, too, I fancy. Am I right?"

"Yes."

"You said, a few months ago, and with some emphasis, that it was unlikely that you would ever marry."

"And was told by your grandmother that I should soon grow out of such foolish pronouncements."

"And have you? Because I think we might make a good thing of it. You said we were both haunted. Together, I think we might let the ghosts rest and find a new purpose in life. I'm very fond of you, as you must know by now. I'd do my best to make you happy. And I think your eyes have been saying much the same thing to me lately. Am I mistaken?"

"No, you're not mistaken. Just now, when I thought you were going away, a dreadful black pit seemed to be opening under my feet."

He smiled and took her in his arms, kissing her gently and holding her close to him.

"The old love? How much does it still mean?" he asked.

She thought for a moment, searching for the truth.

"It's become remote, these past months. A dream of my salad days. As you said, dreams leave you hungry. Now," she said, lifting his hand to her cheek, "there's nothing I want more than to build a new life with you."

"I hope you know what you're taking on," he replied, half smiling as he kissed her again. "I don't know that I can live up to your romantic ideals. I've lived too long in the rough, tough world."

"I'm not worried."

"That's what I love you for. Did you know? Your zest. You get up from the tumbles and carry on with undimmed courage and high expectations. It's very endearing."

"Well, I must say that's putting it all in a very flattering light. Isn't this a lovely spot? I'm so glad that it was here that you asked me to marry you. Something lovely, to remember always."

It was symbolic, she thought. The bend in the river. The long straight stretch downstream, where they could see the past, and had been looking back at it too long, perhaps. And the future round the bend, with only glimpses of the river through the overhanging trees, the water reflecting splinters of sunshine through the branches. All to be sought, that way.

"My dear, romantic young love. No prizes for guessing the place you'll choose for our honeymoon."

"And where, my clever one, will that be?"

"Switzerland."

"That will suit very well," she said solemnly.

"Within reach of a Viennese evening?"

"Better and better."

"But this time, we'll be giving it a more realistic ending," he said, his lips twitching.

"Your grandmother will be pleased. Did you know that she more or less instructed me to marry you? A good, sensible match, she said. You needed a woman and a stable home. I would get a good, responsible husband. And Philippe would have a second home."

"I had a few broad hints myself. A very practical woman, my grandmother. I'm glad you followed her instructions," he added wickedly.

"I wasn't all that enthusiastic at the time. It sounded so cold-blooded."

"But it's warmed up since?"

"Very much so."

"I'm lucky. When? As soon as your job here ends and we can find somewhere to live?"

"Yes. And that won't be easy."

"We'll start straight away."

They stayed by the river until tea-time, when Antonia felt obliged to go in search of Philippe. They met Paul coming away from the Hall, and told him of their engagement. He seemed delighted, and fell in with Pierre's suggestion for a little celebratory dinner for the four of them that night at a country hotel he favoured.

When Janet arrived home just after Pierre had left, she, too, received the news with apparent pleasure, but Antonia sensed something else, too. Surprise? Reservations? But at the lively dinner party that evening, when Paul and Janet toasted their happiness in champagne, she dismissed the idea. Janet had probably been tired after her day at the hospital.

They used Pierre's car that night, and when he deposited them back at the lodge soon after eleven o'clock, Antonia, not wanting the day to end, said,

"She we stroll across to the river before you go, Pierre? It's such a lovely night. I need to walk off that dinner."

Paul and Janet declined to join them, and said goodnight. Pierre took her arm, and they walked round the meadow and through the rose garden. There had been a record crowd visiting Belmont Hall that day. Now it lay sleeping in the moonlight, its terrace deserted, an incongruous red plastic bag, that had escaped the vigilance of the caretaker, staining the flight of steps that led from the terrace to the lawn. Antonia picked it up and deposited it in the bin by some bushes. They crossed the lawn, took the footpath through the woodland and emerged on to the smooth grass walk overlooking the river valley. Pierre leaned on the balustrade, and Antonia remembered her first visit here, when she had been angered by his dismissal of her, by his bored detachment. The night was warm and still. She heard a fox bark in the distance. His arm came round her as she leaned beside him.

"Happy?"

"Wonderfully happy."

He fell silent again, and glancing at his profile, austere in the moonlight, she thought of his observation, "I hope you know what you're taking on." In fact, she was well aware that there was much of Pierre Valais that she did not know. Hidden depths that he did not share with her. Of his affection for her, she had no doubt. Of her own love for him, she had no doubt, either. On those two realities, her confidence in the future was founded. Together they would grow to a deeper understanding of each other.

He turned and cupped her face between his hands. Then he kissed her lingeringly. Afterwards, he caught her to him, roughly.

"I want you, Tonie. I've been alone too long."

"We're neither of us alone any longer," she murmured as his dark head blotted out the pale, moon-washed sky.

8

Reactions

JONATHAN, ARRIVING THE next afternoon for the last of his
tutorials with Philippe, met Antonia's excited announce-
ment with a blink and a frown as he emerged from his
shabby old car.

"You're what?" he said, as though she spoke a foreign
language.

"Pierre Valais and I are engaged to be married. He asked
me yesterday."

"Good grief! Really?"

"Well, you don't think I'm joking, do you? Is it so
incredible?"

"Oh no. Good lord, no. Just that I never thought of you
getting married, settling down. You're always on the move.
Can't see you in a domestic setting, somehow. He's a good
deal older than you, isn't he?"

"Nine years. I don't see that that has anything to do with
it," said Antonia, dampened by Jonathan's attitude,
although she might have expected it.

"Oh well, all the best. Hope it'll work out all right. Told
the parents?"

"No. Don't say anything to them. I'll tell them myself
when I come home on Saturday."

"Righto. Going to be another scorcher. A lot to get into
our last day. Hope young Philippe's ready."

"He's worked well, I think, considering the temptations of the lovely weather and the country here. Are you pleased with his progress?"

"Yes. He's not done badly at all. Quite a good brain, when he concentrates."

And that was all that was said on the matter of Antonia's engagement. Watching her brother's lanky figure striding across the lawn ahead of her, she wondered whether he would in future induce in his pupils the same sense of inferiority which he had always induced in her. Perhaps he ruled a line between those intellectually worthy of his attention and the rest, whom he ignored. Even when they were children, he had been a cool, aloof little boy, and at a very early stage had made it clear that he regarded her as a silly, emotional girl, and at no stage later had he appeared to change that opinion. Cold-blooded, and unreachable. He was going off to Greece at the end of the week for a month's touring holiday on his own before returning to Cambridge. She knew that he would have nothing to tell her about it when he got back. And always this cool repulsion of any news she wanted to share with him, as though he could not bear ever to get involved.

She sighed. Perhaps he came alive with other intellectuals. As far as she was concerned, his knack of making her feel foolish and inadequate was unerring.

She made her way to the refreshment room, where an absentee from the staff was causing hold-ups. The car park was full, a queue was forming for the next conducted tour of the Hall, and the grounds were dotted with people strolling slowly across the sun-baked lawns, lingering in the rose garden, or making for the shade of the woodland. And every garden seat in view was occupied by tired sightseers.

Behind the tea-urn in the refreshment room, the heat was fierce, but she was glad to take part in the lively activity there to offset the chill of Jonathan's reaction to her news.

In the cool of the evening, when it was nearly dark and

the visitors had all gone, Janet joined her for a stroll in the grounds, and she, too, was not as enthusiastic about Antonia's prospects as she might have been.

"Isn't it a little bit hasty, Tonie? You've only known each other for a few months, after all."

"We've no doubts at all."

"You're so much younger than Pierre. Oh, I don't mean only in years. I don't believe in girls getting married when they're young, before they've had time to live their own lives. Afterwards, it's too late. You're trapped into living other people's lives. Your husband's. Your children's. It may be what you want, but you need to have lived long enough as an individual to know whether you want to stop having a life of your own and work of your own choosing."

"Pierre and I are happy together. We haven't either of us been happy on our own for a long time. I know what the loss of his wife meant to him. Or, at least, I've a good idea. Nobody can know who hasn't experienced that kind of bereavement. Now, we've a lot to give to each other."

"You have a lot to give, Tonie. Too much, perhaps, for your own good. What really matters to Pierre, you know, is music. Like Paul with this place, it's his obsession. They have more in common than you might think, Paul and Pierre. You could be left on the perimeter of his life, and yet be tied enough to prevent you from making a life of your own. Is that going to satisfy you?"

"How can you judge, from the outside?"

"I'm judging from my own experience. That's all we ever have to go on. I loved Paul. I do still love him. But if I could go back, I wouldn't marry. I'd live my own life. A man marries and keeps his own life, with added comforts. A woman marries, and loses any life of her own," concluded Janet bitterly.

"I'm sorry," said Antonia unhappily. "But companionship, support, belonging. Surely they count."

"Some men are wedded to their work. I'm only warning you that Pierre could be the same. Think carefully before that wedding ring binds you."

They walked along in silence until Janet, glancing at Antonia's troubled face, said quickly, "Forgive me. I don't like playing Cassandra. Didn't mean to, really. Your news caught me at a bad time. I've had to turn down the chance of being a Superintendent Physiotherapist in a London hospital. I've just posted the letter. Feeling badly about it. I would so much have liked to accept."

"I'm sorry. Would it be quite impossible?"

"Yes. I've been fighting it out with myself for the past week. But it would mean living in London. A full time, responsible job. You know how Paul is wrapped up in this place. And there's Philippe. No, it would be impossible. To have a career, Tonie, you have to be willing to sacrifice other people as well as making sacrifices yourself. That's where women are handicapped. The tradition of putting husbands, children, first is too strong for them. So . . . you can't have two vocations. You must choose. And the moment of choice comes usually when you've had too little experience to make a wise judgment. Hence my Cassandra act."

"But I've no special vocation. No gifts."

"Then, for you, it's simpler. And I hope Pierre makes you very happy. He's a lucky man. You are a life-enhancer. That's a very special gift. Pay no attention to my lecture. Dangerous to think one knows best for other people, anyway. I just had to come out with it, I guess. When that letter went into the box, I felt all life draining out of me. I'll come round."

"What did Paul say about it?"

"That I must make my own decision. He knew what that must be."

"Later on . . . Paul and Philippe. There are compensations."

"Yes. If I can subdue my ego. Philippe's a dear boy. I'm very fond of him. In fact, he's more of a companion than Paul these days," added Janet drily.

*   *   *

Her parents greeted the news with less surprise than her brother.

"I thought that might be the way things were when Pierre last brought you home. He seems a responsible person, and his family, of course, is well known to your grandmother. I'm very glad, dear. And relieved," said her mother briskly, collecting the coffee cups.

"Relieved?"

"That it's not some weird child of light, or whatever they call themselves, or a Marxist revolutionary met on your travels. You've been away from home so much that we've no idea what sort of friends you've made. I'm very glad that you've chosen to settle down with a man mature enough to look after you."

"Hope you'll both be very happy, my dear," said her father, kissing her. Then he went out into the garden.

"Pierre's coming over this afternoon. We thought we'd go and see Grandma after tea," said Antonia.

"Good idea. She'll approve, I'm sure. We're driving Jonathan to the airport this afternoon. We'll probably be back by five, though. How that boy is going to manage for a month on the contents of that one small rucksack of his, I can't imagine."

"He won't need many clothes in Greece at this time of year."

Her mother stopped at the door, tray in hand, as though struck by an afterthought.

"Are you thinking of a long engagement?"

"No. We shall get married before Christmas, if we can find a house."

"I expect you'll prefer a quiet wedding, dear, won't you?

You've never been a girl for a lot of fuss. And with such an enormous family as ours, it has to be all or nothing."

"We haven't discussed it, but I expect that's what Pierre will prefer."

"Very sensible, too. I must just see if Jonathan's got everything he wants. Perhaps you'd wash the coffee cups, Tonie. I'm rather pushed for time this morning. We have to have an early lunch, to get Jonathan to the airport in good time."

"Yes, of course," said Antonia a little blankly, and followed her mother into the kitchen.

At least, she thought, her grandmother would welcome the news with genuine warmth and interest. As indeed she did in her own dignified way.

"There is no one I would sooner welcome to our family than a Valais," she said, after she had embraced them both.

"My grandfather would have approved, too," said Pierre, his eyes gleaming as he met Mirabel's.

"Yes. It would have made him very happy. An old tie of friendship cemented in this way. It's been swift, this coming together. You've travelled a long way, Antonia, since last May."

Mirabel's dark blue eyes regarded her thoughtfully, and Antonia fancied they held a question.

"To a new country," she replied happily, "and the old one seems very dim and barren."

"What odd tricks life plays," said her grandfather. "To have a Valais in the family, after all these years. Eh, Mirrie?"

"The reinforcement of the small element of French blood in our family will be all to the good, I'm sure."

"A little more leavening to the prosaic Rainwood blood, you mean?" said Charles Rainwood with an unaccustomed note of tartness in his voice.

Mirabel smiled and patted his arm, amused that even

now, well into his eighties, the old jealousy of Louis Valais could still put an edge on his tongue.

"I mean that Pierre and Antonia have much to give each other. We must have a special wine with our supper tonight, dear, to drink to their happiness. Can you find one? We don't carry much stock these days."

"What are we eating?"

"Fresh grapefruit. Cold chicken and salad. Cheese and fruit."

"I'll see what we've got in the way of wine, then," said Charles Rainwood, and left them.

"Perhaps you'd go and give him a hand, Antonia. He finds the stairs difficult now."

"Of course, Grandma," said Antonia, and followed her grandfather through the large old-fashioned kitchen, where she was delayed a few minutes by Gwen, the cheerful little Welsh woman who had been part of the household for as long as Antonia could remember. Then she dived down the stairs leading to the cellar, where she knew that her grandfather would spend some considerable time deciding which wine would be most suitable. It was possible, she thought, that her grandmother had manoeuvred them out of the way so that she could have a few quiet words alone with Pierre. There had been that sort of look in her eyes. She wondered what they were talking about . . .

*　　*　　*

"You're looking, and sounding, a very different person from the one I saw at the beginning of the summer, Pierre. I'm so glad, my dear. The bitterness and grief had lasted long enough."

"Yes. Tonie's brought me back to life. She's so full of life herself, it spills over."

"There's a big gap in years between you."

"No handicap."

"Possibly all to the good. Antonia needs a steadying hand."

But she'll want to be treated as an equal, and not as a nice, bright child to cheer your days."

"Now, *Marraine*," protested Pierre. "Is that kind?"

"I would just like you to confirm, my dear, that you are not offering Antonia the shell of yourself."

He walked to the window and stared out at the garden, then said slowly. "I'm very fond of her. I think I can make her happy. That will be my endeavour, anyway."

"She's very much in love with you."

"Let's be realistic. For both of us, this is a second chance. A good chance. It's important to both of us. You need not worry on that account, *Marraine*."

"That is all I wanted to know. You see, Pierre, you can hurt Antonia far more than she can hurt you. I expect, knowing your intelligence, that you have already learned for yourself that she is not nearly so confident and invulnerable as she appears."

"That goes for most of us."

"More for some than others. And lately, Antonia has been haunted by a sense of failure. Unwarranted, I'm sure. She jokes about it. But underneath, the damage is there. Induced, to a certain extent, I'm afraid, by her upbringing. My daughter has a brilliant son. Intellectually, that is. And she has centred her whole life on him, having little time or patience for Antonia."

"Yes, I've noticed the emphasis on the one or two occasions when I've been there. Her father?"

"Cold-blooded, detached, like his son. It's not my way to criticise other people behind their backs, and indeed I've made my views known to my daughter, but I think you, as Antonia's future husband, should know. Because Antonia, herself, would never reveal it. Self-pity has no place in her make-up. But the damage to her self-confidence is there, for all the brave show. A happy marriage will remedy it. Anything less will spread the damage. She will always blame herself for her inadequacies. They've been so inculcated by her family."

"I think she's a more robust character than you might think."

"Brave. Naturally high-spirited. But there are the deeper layers, too, that it is important to understand."

"You think I'm not concerned about those?"

"I think you may not suspect the nature of them. After all, I've known Antonia from birth. Have watched her grow up. Know her family circumstances. That is why I say you can hurt her far more than she can hurt you. You, my dear," she added gently, "have already been hurt almost beyond endurance. That has left callouses where the scars were. It is natural and right that you should seek someone young and gay like Antonia to bring light into your life again, and I shall pray for your happiness."

"Thank you. I promise you, I'm not using Tonie for light relief. I'm not that calloused."

"Forgive me, Pierre, if I gave the impression that I thought you were. When one is old, it is difficult not to be didactic. It's because the happiness of you two young people means so much to me that I try to lay down a few guiding lines. So foolish of me. As if the young ever listen. I never did. You have to learn it all for yourselves. The deeper the understanding you have of each other, though, the greater the chance of happiness in marriage, which needs all the understanding we can muster for its well-being."

"I'm not without experience," said Pierre in a detached tone.

"And I am reproved, which is probably good for me. And in case you think my view of Antonia is out of focus, and my concern for her unflattering to you, I must add that she is a most impetuous, headstrong girl in many ways, and that your firm, restraining hand will be invaluable to her."

"*Marraine*, I am comforted," declared Pierre with gay panache as he lifted her hand and kissed it.

His black eyes were dancing now, daring her to lecture further, his mood mischievous. How like Louis he was, she thought. The same pride, which she had pricked. The same quick changes of mood. The sound of laughter from Antonia in the hall brought a smile to their lips, and Mirabel said, "Welcome to our family, Pierre. I shall drink to the new member with heartfelt happiness. Nobody could be more welcome than the grandson of Louis Valais."

*　　*　　*

The reaction from Pierre's grandmother was on a slightly different level. Her letter to Antonia arrived at the end of the following week, written in firm, spiky writing on thin paper.

My dear Antonia,

I have today written to Pierre congratulating him on your engagement, and now I would like to add a few lines just for you. Naturally, I am delighted with the news. If it had come sooner, I should have asked Pierre to take Philippe into his care, but as you tell me that the boy has settled in very happily with Paul and Janet, I am content in the knowledge that you will be able to provide a second home for him. His letters have pleased me very much. Thank you, my dear, for helping him to adapt so successfully to his new life.

I have no need to tell you that I find this a good, sensible marriage, and I hope you will quickly find a suitable home. Pierre will be a good husband, and you will learn how to handle him as I learned how to handle his grandfather. When the temper flares, passive resistance is the line I advise. Do not be weak with him. You will manage very well, I am sure, and make a happy, well-run home for Pierre and your children.

It disappoints me that I cannot travel far now, and

shall not be able to come to your wedding, but I shall look forward to seeing you both here whenever possible.

My regards to your esteemed grandparents,

Yours sincerely,

Marguerite Valais.

"What did yours say?" asked Antonia when she saw Pierre that evening.

"Not much. My grandmother, as you know, is not given to flowery sentiments. Very pleased. Wishes us happiness. I've made a good choice. That's about all. I didn't bother to bring it."

In fact, it had been made so clear that the old lady saw this as a marriage of convenience that Pierre had thought it tactless to produce the letter and had torn it up.

"Well, I'm glad I shall know what to do when the temper flares."

"And me, the mildest of men!"

"As mild as ginger."

"Grossly unfair. She doesn't tell *me* how to cope when your temper flares. And my hair's not red," said Pierre, fingering an odd strand that had escaped at the nape of her neck.

"I wish mine wasn't. I've often thought of dyeing it, but that wouldn't make it any more manageable."

"Don't you dare. It's beautiful hair. Warm and glowing, like a fire on a cold night. *'Est-elle brune, blonde ou rousse?'* Verlaine asked that in a poem, I remember. My choice is *rousse* every time."

He had untied the flat bow and was passing his hand under the shining, rippling strands of her hair, his fingers brushing the nape of her neck, and she shivered. Then he turned her round and caught her tightly to him.

"*Mignonne,*" he murmured, his lips brushing hers. "You're happy?"

She could not begin to tell him how happy she was.

When, a little later, they walked on along the river bank, she watched the leaves drifting down from the overhanging trees and marvelled at the transformation in her life since those same leaves were unfurling, tender and green, in the spring. The reception to the news of their engagement might have seemed, on the whole, luke-warm, but to Antonia it had opened up a whole new and lovely landscape where the sun shone warmly all the time.

9

Willows' End

THE HOT DAYS of August ended in storms and high winds at the beginning of September, to be succeeded by calm, fine days and cool nights.

Philippe started school, supported by his friend, Tom, who was luckily in the same form, and quickly took to his new life. Antonia, her task ended, agreed to continue working at Belmont Hall, helping out in the refreshment room and the little shop where guide books and photographs were sold, until the end of October, when the visitors tailed off, but she insisted on moving to lodgings at the head gardener's cottage.

"But why move at this stage? You'll be getting married as soon as you find somewhere to live, and you're more than welcome to stay with us until then," said Janet one evening as they were picking some plums in the lodge garden.

"You're very kind, but two's company. I think you and Paul need your home to yourselves and Philippe. The family unit."

"You've helped."

"Not any longer. I'm a buffer. Keeping you from coming out with it when I'm there. And it's better for you to have sole charge of Phil now."

"Well, if you say so," said Janet doubtfully.

"I shall be around just the same. And I get on very well

with the Septimers. They'll be glad of a lodger for a few months. Since their daughter married, the empty bedroom depresses them, they say."

"Mrs. Septimer's nice enough, but can anyone get on well with old Luke Septimer? He's about as forthcoming as a lump of granite."

"I adore him," said Antonia, smiling. "He might have grown out of the ground himself. Do you suppose he sleeps in that trilby hat?"

"You'll have a chance to find out if he wears it for breakfast, anyway."

And so it was settled, and Antonia moved her few belongings to the cottage in the lane just outside the boundary wall of the estate.

She spent most of her free time with Pierre house-hunting, but nothing suitable turned up until at the end of the month they went to see a house a few miles down the river valley which had been put on the market by an acquaintance of Paul's.

"It's a broken-down place," Paul had said. "Neglected for years. The owner used to spend most of his time abroad. Now he's taken himself off to Jersey, and left it in the hands of the agents. May be beyond restoring, but it's in a nice position with a decent piece of land. Can't be sold to developers. It's in a protected area. So the price ought to be fairly reasonable."

They found it with difficulty, as it was quite concealed from the lane, and the entrance was so overgrown with hazel trees that Pierre drove past once without noticing it. They were directed back again by the barman of the nearest village inn, and parked the car under the hazel trees. They found the wide white gate, permanently open because it was off its rusty hinges, half hidden by elderberry bushes, but Antonia held some branches back to reveal a name in black letters. Willows' End. They walked up the gravel

drive, which was weed-infested and overgrown on each side
by dense thickets of laurels and holly.

"This will be some dump, I guess," said Pierre.

"Intriguing," said Antonia.

Pierre smiled. She had approached each possibility with
high expectation and enthusiasm in spite of the yawning
gap between agents' descriptions and the realities which had
been revealed on every investigation so far.

The sun was sinking and its rays did not penetrate the
green jungle on each side of them, but at the end, the drive
opened out into a wide gravel area fronting a long, low,
once-white house, with a pedimented porch and regularly
spaced, tall windows, several panes of which were broken,
and some of which were nearly invisible under wreaths of
a vast, crimson creeper.

"I say, this looks exciting," said Antonia.

Pierre lifted the palms of his hands heavenwards and
gave a little shrug, the only mannerism which reminded
Antonia of the French half of his blood.

"I'm full of foreboding," he said. "Just the sort of broken
down, romantic trappings that would appeal to you. I
scent dry rot, bad drains, leaking roof and primitive
plumbing."

It was only with difficulty that he was able to open the
door with the massive key the agent had given him. Inside
it smelled musty, but appeared dry, due, no doubt, observed
Pierre, to the unusually dry, warm summer. Antonia walked
across the large, square hall into the reception rooms. These
were spacious and warmed by the mellow light from the
slanting rays of the sun through the tall windows, which
helped to offset the depressing effect of dirty, torn wall-
papers and dingy ceilings. The kitchen was large and
square, and the only concession to a kitchen unit was one
built-in cupboard from floor to ceiling, the upper half of
which would be quite out of reach without a ladder. At each
end of the house, projecting at right angles, were two wings,

one in the shape of a large conservatory, the other Antonia could only guess might have been a billiard-room. The two wings enclosed a courtyard of dilapidated paving with a plinth in the centre topped by a moss-encrusted urn from which a few wisps of ivy trailed forlornly.

"Yes, it was a billiard-room," said Antonia triumphantly. "Look."

She had been peering inside a cupboard and now brought out a marker board, covered in dust and cobwebs.

"Well done. What do you suppose they grew in that replica of the Crystal Palace?" asked Pierre, looking out of the window across the paved courtyard to the conservatory.

"Oh, ferns and palms and aspidistras. But wouldn't this room be ideal for your music room? It would house your piano and all your records and books. Make a marvellous workroom for you right away from the rest of the house."

But Pierre was examining a dried-out stain on the wall at the corner of the room, his mind evidently only concerned with structural defects.

The wide, curving staircase from the hall to the upper storey led them to four good sized rooms and a mammoth bathroom.

"How extraordinary!" exclaimed Antonia. "You could swim in that bath. Have you ever seen one like that before?"

"Never. The Colonel must have brought it back with him from Singapore. One part of the agents' description is certainly apt. It's a house of character all right."

"I like it. All the light and space. I feel it welcomes us, somehow. Let's have a look at the garden."

The garden was two acres of wilderness, bounded at the end by the river, here little more than a narrow stream almost hidden behind a curtain of willow trees. Whatever shape the garden had taken in the past was now concealed under a jungle of brambles, nettles, and long grass. There were some gnarled old fruit trees, and a hotch-potch of shrubs that had managed to hold their own. And dominating all, an enormous monkey puzzle tree, with all its lower branches dead. Surveying this monstrosity, Pierre said, "No wonder the owner's fled to Jersey."

"But what a challenge!" said Antonia, her eyes shining. "We could make a lovely home of this."

"What would we want a place of this size for?"

"I like space around me. Grand for children, too. That is, if we could afford it, of course," she said, looking at Pierre hopefully.

"We could afford to buy it, but could we afford to make it habitable?"

"We could do it bit by bit. I'd rather have a big shabby place with a big garden than a small, glossy one. Doesn't it appeal to you, Pierre? It has such atmosphere. We could expand here instead of being boxed up. It's different."

"It certainly is that. Victoriana, British Raj, and all. But I'm with you in liking space around me."

Her eyes sparkling with enthusiasm, Antonia enlarged on all the possibilities, volunteered to take over the reclaiming of the garden herself, and painted a wonderfully rosy picture of life at Willows' End.

"And you needn't be bothered with any of it. You can just retire to your music room and leave it to me. I don't mind how shabby it has to be. I know it will make a splendid home for us. And you must admit that we've seen nothing so far that would give you anything like a domain of your own for your music," she concluded, seeing this as her trump card.

"What makes you think I wouldn't want to be bothered with it? One of us has to keep our feet on the ground, though," he said with a smile, putting his arm round her shoulders.

"I'm a great believer in first impressions, in intangibles, where houses are concerned. This felt right to me as soon as I saw it. I could see our lives here. Plenty of light and space, and the country to look out on. Dogs and children.

We could all be happy here without being under each other's feet. Do you think I'm crazy?" she asked anxiously, longing for him to agree with her.

"In a nice way. Hope the surveyor's report isn't too catastrophic. As a matter of fact, it looks pretty solidly built. We'll put down a deposit and have it, subject to surveyor's report."

When she turned her happy, glowing face to him, he kissed her and she held him tightly. Afterwards, as it grew dark, they wandered again through the rooms, and then once more down to the river.

"The first thing we'll do is to have that monkey puzzle tree cut down," said Pierre as they picked their way through the garden, unhooking brambles, dodging nettles, stumbling in the dim light over unsuspected obstacles hidden in the long, tangled grass.

"So much to plan. Won't it be exciting?"

He smiled and agreed, wondering if they were both crazy, but knowing that to her, difficulties would only be a challenge in a great adventure, and warmed by her eager, ardent spirit.

Antonia, watching the moon rise above the willows, was seeing the future. I shall make a happy home here for Pierre and our children, she thought. A home where they will all feel free, but belonging, united by love. It will be a citadel against the world, where we shall feel safe and cared for. Where I can put down roots and have a worth-while end to all the efforts I mean to put into it. I've found the right road at last, with no dead end, but leading on and widening out. All the old feeling of frustration and failure had vanished, and she leaned her head against Pierre's shoulder, deeply happy, as she had never been before.

10

The Other World

A FEW EVENINGS later, Antonia walked along the footpath leading to the fruit farm to meet some friends who were visiting Pierre that day. They were coming, he had explained, to discuss a school of music now being built with funds from a Trust set up by Pierre and his wife just before her death. He had never mentioned his wife's name to her before this, and had been brief in his reference to the Trust. It was the first time she had heard about it. He was taking his friends out to dinner that evening, and had invited her to meet them.

In spite of the fact that it was nearly dark when she arrived, Kevin Ryton was still at work in the orchard, picking apples.

"Short of labour, and we want to catch the early market," he said.

He was a burly, good-natured man, with a simple, friendly way with him that Antonia liked and felt at home with. They were a contrasting pair, he and Pierre. Like a good, steady cart-horse teamed up with a nervy, intelligent race-horse. But they seemed to get on very well together. Pierre lived in one half of the rambling farm house, Kevin in the other, and they shared a dining-room. They were catered for by a daily woman from the village during the week, and messed for themselves at weekends. She was glad he was getting married to the pleasant-faced woman who was the local doctor's receptionist, and whose comforting, soothing manner, Janet said, was invaluable to nervy patients and children. One could confidently predict a serene if not exciting partnership.

She left him to his task and walked round the farm house to the side entrance, aware of a slight reluctance to face these friends of Pierre who came from his old life of music in which she had played no part. A world almost unknown to her. She found them having drinks and discussing plans spread out over a table in the large living-room at the back of the house. Pierre looked up with a smile as she hovered in the doorway.

"Ah, there you are, darling. Come and meet my friends. Joan Midway, the secretary and driving force of the Trust. David Penryn, an old friend of my teaching days at the college of music."

Antonia was conscious of being keenly scrutinised by Joan Midway, a thin, dark-haired woman, with an intelligent face and a rather intense manner which gave no concessions to conventional platitudes. Antonia guessed her to be in her late thirties. She had an authoritative manner which made Antonia feel that she was back in the schoolroom facing the headmistress, and the verdict in those judging eyes, she felt, was not altogether favourable.

"This is a day of surprises," she said with a smile that did not reach her eyes. "Having at last tracked Pierre down after all his travels and found him holed up on a fruit farm, of all places, he now springs his engagement on us. He only told us five minutes ago."

"And I'm sure we wish you both all the happiness in the world," said David Penryn quickly.

Antonia smiled and thanked him, and after a few minutes of general conversation they turned their attention to the plans again, and Antonia watched and listened. She gathered that the plans were of a centre for singing and operatic study, and that David Penryn was the guiding light. He had a pleasing personality and a distinguished appearance. A tall, well-built man, with thick greying hair, handsome features and a mellifluous voice, his keen interest in the venture was evident. Joan Midway, incisive, alert, was no less enthusiastic.

"A fitting memorial to Claire," she declared. "We want to call it the Claire Valais School, Pierre. Subject to your consent, of course."

"I don't think that would have been Claire's choice," said Pierre slowly, "but if that is your wish, I've no objection."

"I think it's right that it should be so," said David Penryn quietly.

"So be it," said Pierre.

Antonia wondered whether this discussion was painful to him. His manner was thoughtful, controlled. She could not read his expression, only saw his eyes narrow as Joan Midway said reproachfully, "We've missed your advice all this time, Pierre. You should have been in on it before."

"I knew when we set up the Trust that it would be in good hands."

"But we need you. I'm sure we can count on you to accept the position of Director. You're too valuable to be lost. On the administrative side and the teaching side, we need you. I'm really amazed that you need time to think it over," concluded Joan, her eyes resting momentarily on Antonia.

"The architect's done a good job. Now let's think of dinner," said Pierre, rolling up the plans.

He drove them to the same country hotel where they had celebrated their engagement, but Antonia was again relegated to the role almost of onlooker, as it was music and the school that they discussed most of the time. Pierre now and again tried to draw her into the conversation, turn it to other topics, but always Joan Midway brought it back to music, the old days when Pierre taught, the days of Claire's success in opera, the school they were building in her memory. Antonia, herself occasionally reproved by Mirabel Rainwood for lack of tact, felt that she was a very mild offender compared with Joan Midway. No amount of thoughtlessness would have made her eulogise the late wife of a man in the presence of his fiancée, nor make the latter feel so excluded as to cause her to wonder if she was invisible.

Herself a frank and friendly talker, she was that evening often reduced to scanning the other diners in the room, or watching the waiters cooking exotic dishes over the naked flame of a spirit stove. She wondered if they ever poured too much brandy into the frying pan before setting it alight for the flambé dishes, and decided to try it herself some time, and emulate their dexterity.

The evening dragged, and she was glad when they drove back to the farm house, and she could busy herself making a last pot of tea before Pierre's friends went. She wanted the comfort of Pierre's arms round her. Wanted to lose this feeling of being shut out.

After the tea, Joan asked Pierre to play for them.

"Let us hear something from you before we go, Pierre, to crown the evening," she said.

Pierre smiled and shrugged, then opened the grand piano in the far corner of the room. He sat looking at the keys for a moment, then played a Liszt sonata. Antonia had never heard him play before. Even with her limited knowledge, she recognised a fine talent, appreciated the power and technical mastery of his playing. But the music was sad, she thought. Heart-tugging. At times, fiercely despairing. She watched his absorbed face, his wonderfully supple but strong fingers, loving him, aching for him, conscious that he was in another world.

They were silent for a moment or two after he had finished, then Joan thanked him gently, adding with a note of emotion in her voice which surprised Antonia, "You haven't lost any of your skill or your marvellous sensitivity, Pierre. You can't bury such talent."

"There are more avenues than one. Watch out for my BBC scripts. And translating the libretti of operas is a useful task, after all," he said lightly.

Antonia saw Joan's eyes go round the room, taking in the large record cabinet, the crammed bookshelves, the desk and typewriter, the tape recorder, the pile of music, the piano.

"Yes, you're busy enough, I can see. I'm relieved that the farming was only a temporary little side-line. I was afraid from the way you spoke over the phone that you'd gone mad and retired into a peasant's existence."

And, for the first time that evening, Antonia saw Pierre's patience with Joan's didactic manner evaporate, and a flicker of anger lit his eyes as he said with the old mocking silkiness which had once riled her and which now he never used towards her, "And you thought it your duty to bring me back to sanity? But we all have our own ideas about sanity, Joan dear."

She flushed a little, and stood up, saying briskly, "I hate to see talent wasted. And you must admit that we had cause to be worried. You just disappeared from our lives, after all those years of working together, of friendship."

"He needed to get away," broke in David Penryn. "Very understandable. It's good to have you back now, though, Pierre. You'll think over our suggestion? You're so right for the job."

"I'll let you know next week, but I think it unlikely that I'll accept, although I appreciate your confidence in me. My life's taken a different direction, that's all."

"Claire would have wished it," said Joan harshly, then, as she saw the dangerous light in Pierre's eyes, she added quickly, "But we'll be hoping, anyway. And thank you for a splendid day, and letting us hear you play again."

"Good to see you both. I'm grateful for all the hard

work and enthusiasm you're putting into the project. Now I'll just get my car out of the way, David. It's blocking yours at the moment. Be back in a few minutes."

He went out, and Joan fetched her coat from the hall. Antonia collected the tea-things and carried them out to the kitchen, wanting to escape from the tension she could sense. Then she took her own coat and slipped out of the side door, in need of some fresh air. It was a dark, moonless sky, pricked with stars, and the air was cool and sweet with the spicy fragrance of some chrysanthemums nearby. She could hear the crunch of the car wheels on the gravel as Pierre moved his car out to the lane. Then from the open window behind her, she heard Joan Midway's clipped voice.

"I can't understand Pierre hesitating for a moment. He's made for the job. It was Claire's money that set it up. His talent, his musicianship, would help to make it one of the finest training centres for young singers. He can't refuse."

"I think he may," said David Penryn slowly.

"I can't believe it. It must be that girl who's making him hesitate. What can have possessed him to have tied himself up with a young girl who obviously doesn't know the first thing about music when his whole life has been devoted to it? She wouldn't like living in London, he said. An outdoor, country type. It's so incongruous. What can he be thinking of?"

"He withdrew from the active world of music some years ago. He changed, after Claire's death. It's not for us to judge what's right for him."

"Oh, of course he wanted time to get over it. I understand that. But to marry right out of his own country a girl years younger than himself. After *Claire*. An affaire, perhaps. Understandable. But marriage, and settling down to a domestic life in the country with a girl who shares none of his love of music, is lunacy. Can't you talk to him, David? You and he are such old friends."

"Pierre is a man who makes up his own mind, Joan. I'll do what I can when we meet next week."

"Do you suppose he's yielded to some passing attraction, and now feels bound to go through with it? You know that streak of old-fashioned chivalry in him."

"How can we judge from the outside? Antonia is a nice girl. It's not for us to say that they won't be happy together."

"It is, you know. Pierre will be trying to fit himself into a mould which was never made for him. Do you suppose she's open to persuasion? I wonder whether I could get her alone some time and make her see the situation. Persuade her to encourage him to accept the position and take up his proper place in London musical circles. If there have to be sacrifices, surely she should make them. Most wives, after all, have to adapt themselves to their husbands' careers. It's a question of priorities."

"Don't interfere, Joan. You could do more harm than good. Pierre wouldn't thank either of us for that. He makes his own decisions. He's a complex character, you know, and won't brook interference in his private life."

"But people with talent owe something to the outside world."

"He's using it in other directions now."

"Oh, you're so defeatist, David! Anyone would think you don't mind one way or the other about Pierre being Director of the centre."

"I do care, very much. But the decision must be Pierre's. We'll see what happens next week."

"Well, I never thought we'd be going back without his enthusiastic acceptance. How can he contemplate marrying Antonia whatever-her-name-is after a wonderful person like Claire? He shouldn't marry again. He should give his life to music and the centre set up in her memory."

"We haven't all got your single-minded fervour, Joan," said David Penryn's voice a little drily.

"But it's all such a waste. He doesn't have to marry to have a normal sex life. He's not a child. But the centre of his life is music, and always will be. Claire was part of it, in a way no other woman could be, let alone a young ignoramus like this one."

"Keep your voice down, Joan. No use getting exasperated because people won't do as you want them to do. Anyway, Pierre hasn't refused yet."

Steps on the gravel drive made Antonia dive round the house back into the kitchen, shaken and distressed. She took a few minutes to get herself in hand before joining the others in the hall. Pierre gave her a searching look, but she was able to chat cheerfully to David Penryn as they walked out to his car. Standing beside Pierre, waving them off, she was surprised to find her knees shaking so much that they would hardly support her.

"Feeling all right, Tonie? You looked pale in the hall."

"Quite all right. A bit tired."

"Must have been rather boring for you, this evening. I'd forgotten what an obsessive woman Joan Midway is. Gets her teeth into a subject and won't let it go. Like a terrier with a bone. I wanted you to meet David, though. A good friend of mine."

"He's very likeable."

"We'll have him on his own next time. You're trembling. Cold?"

"A bit shivery."

He took her in his arms and kissed her gently, then kept his arm round her shoulders as they walked down the drive to his car in the lane. On the short drive back, he seemed preoccupied, and Antonia tried to sort out her troubled thoughts. She felt inadequate, a prey to the inferiority complex which had dogged her through the last few years. She kept hearing the contemptuous words of Joan Midway, "let alone a young ignoramus like this one".

When Pierre drew up outside the gardener's cottage on

the boundary of the Belmont Hall estate, she turned to him.

"This post of Director of the school. Will you accept it?"

"Almost certainly not. I've other plans," he said briefly.

"You know, if you liked the idea, I'd be willing to live in London to make it practical," she said diffidently.

"Right out of your element, my dear. You'd be utterly miserable."

And she knew he was right. It would be like going to prison.

"I wouldn't like to feel I was stopping you from doing something you want to do."

"Put it out of your mind, dear. I've a lot of work on hand. I shan't go back to teaching. I'll hold a watching brief. Take an interest, of course."

"This Trust. You've never mentioned it before. But you're a trustee."

"In a minor capacity only. The others, David, Joan and an accountant friend of mine, are all very capable and keen people. They were chosen carefully. I can safely leave things to them. Now you'd better rustle up a hot drink before you go to bed. You're still shivering," he said, taking her hand.

When he kissed her goodnight, she suddenly tightened her hands round his shoulders and returned his kiss with a kind of despairing ardour, then buried her face against his jacket.

"Why, *mignonne*," he said gently, "you're all of a dither. What is it? Nothing's wrong, is it?"

"No. Of course not. I just want to make sure you're here," she said, her voice muffled.

"Very much here," he said, laying a hand on her hair. "And, by the way, I heard from the surveyor today. He won't be able to do the survey for a couple of weeks, but he'll fix it for mid-October."

Antonia sat up and tried to push away the feeling that a huge gap had opened up between them that evening, saying as cheerfully as she could, "Well, now that I've met your friends, you must return the compliment and meet some of mine. Jean Brynton phoned me today. She and Darrel are having a few friends to dinner next Friday, and want me to bring you. Nick's going, and Marcus and Lucy Wicklow, those friends I made at the other job I had at a stately home. I told you about them, remember? Marcus works at Darrel's Horticultural Station now."

"I remember. I'd very much like to meet them, but Friday's the night I'm committed to this trustees' meeting in London."

"Oh no! Couldn't they change the night?"

"Afraid not. David's away all next week, rehearsing and conducting an oratorio in a Suffolk church. He won't be back until Friday afternoon. And the other trustee is only free on Friday evening. I can't skip it, because there are decisions to make about an alteration to the plans, too, as well as settling the question of Director. Sorry. We must make another opportunity soon. Invite them over here."

"You'd like them all, I know."

"Is this your first meeting with Darrel since we came back from Switzerland?"

"Oh, it's ages since I saw him and Jean. Jean was very reproachful. She'd only heard about our engagement at second-hand, from Nick. I was told off."

"Any qualms? About meeting Darrel."

"No. Like you, my life has taken another direction. They're awfully pleased about our engagement. Want to meet you."

"I've a lot to live up to. Better see this hero of yours, and see what I'm up against. We'll fix a date before the month's out. It really has stopped hurting?"

"What? Darrel, you mean?"

"What else?"

"I haven't thought about him for weeks. Yes, it's stopped hurting. Just good to know that he and Jean are my friends, and will be yours, too, I hope."

"You don't think, in the circumstances, it might be better to let sleeping dogs lie? I've found that best myself. To bury the past."

"It was hero-worship belonging to my salad days, Pierre. I've realised that lately. Got it in perspective. It was a dream. I don't need dreams any more."

It was hours before she could get to sleep that night, thinking over the events of that evening, trying not to see the force of Joan Midway's arguments, fighting to keep intact the shining new world which had opened up to her since Pierre had come into her life.

11

Wheeling and Dealing

IF ANTONIA HAD nursed any thought that seeing Darrel again might reopen old wounds, she was completely reassured at the dinner party. The warm liking was there, the respect, but none of the old frustration and longing. Glad to be with her old friends, eager to tell them about Pierre and their future plans, the evening somehow restored her confidence, and when Nick dropped her off at her home on his way to London, she was in high spirits.

"Well, my child," said Nick in his cool, half mocking voice, "I gather you've finished running up those blind alleys you told me about and have found a more promising road."

"Yes. I do wish Pierre could have been with us this evening."

"M'm. He's lost no time since he first put in an appearance at Grandma's tea-party last May."

"That seems a lifetime ago. It's a different world now."

"Always such excess!" sighed Nick.

"Well, it was you who quoted that Spanish proverb, 'There are no birds in last year's nest'. It's so good not to be looking back any more. To be looking ahead."

She knew she need say no more. Although she had never mentioned her long and abortive love for Darrel Brynton, and had thought it her secret alone, she guessed now that this shrewd cousin of hers had been aware of it. After all, he had been with her during that summer in Ireland when it had all started.

He put a hand on her shoulder for a moment.

"I'm glad, Tonie. Pierre's a lucky chap and I hope you'll both be very happy. He looks as though he's got enough mettle to cope with your emotional excesses," he drawled, as though fearing to sound sentimental.

"He's pretty volatile himself. Have you *never* lost your heart? Never even lost your head, Nick?"

"The first, far too dangerous. The second, far too exhausting. I like my peaceful ivory tower."

"Dear Nick. I hope you'll be a frequent visitor to Willows' End. I'm going to have a lovely prowl round it on my own tomorrow. Pierre's bogged down with work this weekend. I suppose you wouldn't care to drive down tomorrow and have a look at it with me?"

He thought for a moment, then said, "All right. My present book is firmly stuck in the mud. An excursion to this remarkable domicile you've found will be a change and perhaps unblock my brain."

"Good. Though I'm sure your brain is never blocked for long. And I may as well tell you now that no cold water which your rational mind may play on our beautiful find will affect me in the slightest. For me, it's the loveliest home I ever saw."

"Poor Pierre! From what you've already told me, it sounds like the ruins of Tintern Abbey with a glasshouse tacked on. I shall be interested to see your folly, my child."

She was still smiling as he drove off. She was very fond of Nick, and was glad he was coming tomorrow. She always found him an amusing companion, and he would help to offset the blankness of a weekend at home without the prospect of seeing Pierre.

*   *   *

For Antonia, back at Belmont Hall the following Monday, it started as any other Monday, with a fine day bringing a good crowd to the house and gardens. In the mellow autumn sunshine, the house and grounds looked their best, and she was kept busy at the shop all the morning, selling photographs and guides. It was nearly lunchtime when a good-looking, slightly built man with dark, wavy hair, asked for a guide book, and gave her a charming smile as she handed it to him. He had white, even teeth and large brown eyes like a spaniel's.

"Is it open at lunch-time? The house, I mean."

"No. Closed between one and three o'clock. But the grounds are worth exploring, and you can get a light lunch at the refreshment room."

"Thanks."

A few minutes later, she locked up the shop and emerged to find the young man lingering in the drive.

"Which direction for the refreshments?" he asked, with the same warm smile.

"Take the right fork. I'm going there myself."

"Good. My luck's in. Nice place, this."

"That's the under-statement of the year."

He laughed and glanced at her with appreciation. Nothing doing, thought Antonia. I'm not in the market for a quick pick-up.

"Worked here long?" he asked.

"This summer."

"Like it?"

"Very much.

"A stately pile all right," he said as they came in sight of the house. "What's the period?"

"Eighteenth century. Wonderful porcelain and pictures inside. The next guided tour is at three o'clock."

"Takes some looking after, I guess. The chap in charge is named Valais, I believe."

"Yes."

"I used to know his brother. Pierre Valais. Lost touch, unfortunately. I wonder if I could get his address from his brother. I'd like to look him up again."

Antonia hesitated. He was pleasant, well-spoken. She did not know why she hesitated. Frank by nature, she saw no reason why she should not help him.

"I can give you his address."

"You know Pierre?"

"I'm engaged to him."

"Well, well! So he's taking the plunge again, is he? Some men have all the breaks," he said as he opened the swing door of the refreshment room for her and surveyed the tables.

It was crowded, and she had no valid reason for refusing to share with him the one vacant table there.

"My luck's in again. Meeting you, and now lunching with you. I'm Stuart Rockland. And you?"

"Antonia Mendyp."

"Soon to be Mrs. Valais. Delighted to meet you, Antonia."

"How long is it since you saw Pierre?"

"Oh, about three or four years, I suppose. How is he? Does he live round here? He used to have a flat in London, but went abroad, I heard."

He had a sympathetic manner, and she talked happily to him about Pierre and the fruit farm, and mentioned Willows' End.

"Sounds delightful."

He was studying her thoughtfully, as though weighing something up, and Antonia dampened down her enthusiasm and said in a practical voice; "Of course, the place has been very neglected. There's a lot to be done to it."

"Well, there's no difficulty about that provided you've got the money, and old Pierre's got plenty of that."

"Has he?"

"Don't you know?"

"We don't discuss it much."

"A sure sign of plenty. Claire made a packet. She would have left it all to Pierre."

"I wouldn't know about that. I do know that some of her money, if not all, has gone into a trust fund to raise a training centre for singers."

"Not all of it, I hope, because some of it is owing to me. Can I fetch you another cup of coffee?"

"No. Yes, please," she added hurriedly, needing time to think.

She watched him go to the counter and wait for the coffee, uneasy now, not knowing quite how to take him. She was no good at finesse, however, and when he returned she said bluntly, "How can it be owing to you? Claire Valais died more than three years ago. Why didn't you claim it?"

"Well, it was a little delicate. I didn't want to press it. Shouldn't now, if I weren't up against it. I hope Pierre will be reasonable and honour her debt to me."

"If he knows about it, he will, I'm sure."

"Oh, he doesn't know the details, and I hope he won't. I shall just ask him to fork up for old times' sake. If that fails, I may have to produce the evidence of the debt."

"Why do you hope he won't know the details?"

"He wouldn't approve."

"I wish you'd be more explicit."

"Claire and I were . . . very attached. Need I say more?" She looked at him incredulously.

"I don't believe you. Pierre was the only man in her life."

"You're very emphatic about a woman you never knew. And touchingly innocent, Antonia. I like you for it. We'll say no more."

"Oh yes, we will. I want to get this straight. Claire Valais, you say, owed you money. How much?"

"Five hundred pounds. Not so much a debt. She'd promised to give it to me."

"What for?"

"A business venture she was anxious to support."

"Why?"

"Shall we say, out of affection?" he said smoothly, with a little smile.

"Were you blackmailing her? Threatening to let Pierre know of your relationship?"

"What unpleasant conclusions you do leap to, Antonia. I don't like such ugly terms. I was embarking on what looked like a promising business venture and I needed a little more capital. Claire was making a lot of money by then. You knew, of course, that she was a successful opera singer? She could spare the money and wanted to help. I'd been tossing up about going abroad when this chance cropped up, and Claire wanted to keep me here. She was working in London then," he concluded, still eyeing her with an odd expression which she found difficult to read but which she most certainly did not like.

"But why bring it up now, after all this time, when Claire is dead? It's not reasonable to expect Pierre to pay up. Did he see you as a close friend?"

"Oh, I was accepted, but I'm afraid he thought me a little feckless. However, this time he may be feeling in a more generous frame of mind, since he's engaged to a delightful and adoring girl, and has Claire's money behind him as well as his own earnings, which are probably comfortable, since he's not without talent and some standing in his precious world of music."

"I don't think any of that would weigh with Pierre if he thought you were feckless."

"Ah, but this time I have a concrete offer to join a friend in the States who's running a country club. I just need that five hundred pounds to pay off a few small debts and give me enough for my air fare. I can produce the offer from America to back my request. I'm not altogether sanguine about my reception, mind you. But it's Claire's money I'm asking for, not his. The money that was promised to me."

"But you can't tell him that without revealing what was between you and Claire. And you're not crazy enough to think that he would pay you the money, knowing that," she said.

"Hardly. But I think I can make a fair case without going that far. Old friends, and all that. If the sky looks cloudy, I may even ask for a loan, though I shouldn't repay it because it really is money Claire promised me."

"And if he refuses?"

"That will be unfortunate. I shall have to produce the evidence of Claire's promise. It might not make him pay up, but it would lend credibility to my case, dent that arrogance of his, and destroy a few illusions."

"What is the evidence?"

"A letter. A very fond letter."

"You couldn't be so cruel! Pierre loved her deeply. He was shattered by her death."

"I'm sure he was. Claire was a very exceptional person. Beautiful, talented, generous and passionate. I loved her very deeply, too."

"Have you been hatching this as a revenge, then?"

"Nothing so melodramatic, Antonia," he said, laughing. "Believe me, I need the money. That's all. But I don't feel called upon to spare Pierre's feelings if he refuses."

There was silence between them for some moments, then she looked up from her cold coffee and said, "I don't believe it. I don't believe Claire was that sort of person. Everybody who knew her thought so much of her. She and Pierre were so happy together. Their work bound them so closely. There wouldn't have been room in her life for another man."

He shrugged his shoulders.

"You *are* an innocent. This isn't Queen Victoria's reign, you know."

"Lies are lies, and double dealing is double dealing in any reign. Show me the proof. I shan't believe you without."

"But you don't have it, Antonia. It's Pierre who will be shown the proof, if he doesn't cough up like a gentleman."

"He won't. You must know as well as I do that he'll need good reason, and is not a man to yield to persuasion against his own judgment."

"I fear you may be right, but so much the worse for him, I'm afraid. And I shan't shed any tears. I shall use what weapons I can to force that money out of him. I must have it. The letter I shall produce may shock him, but it still contains a specific promise from Claire to pay me five hundred pounds. It is owing to me from the money he inherited from her."

"Have you got the letter with you?"

"Naturally. I hope to see him some time today, now that I've tracked him down at last. It was quite by chance that I heard that Paul Valais was in charge of this place, and was able to pick up the trail so easily, with your help."

"Can I see the letter?"

"Well, since you doubt my word, I'll show you part of it. The relevant part. The rest was not meant for anybody else's eyes, but may have to be revealed to Pierre, if he proves difficult."

He took out a folded letter and showed her the second page. The handwriting was firm, with a pronounced forward slope. He held one corner of it while she leaned over and read,

. . . a splendid opportunity and one which will keep you near me. Of course I will gladly give you the five hundred pounds, with my loving hopes for your success. I can't send it today, as I'm waiting for a new cheque book, but it will be along any day now, and you shall have the cheque, I promise.

Can't write much more, as I have been feeling unwell

all this week and Pierre insisted on calling in the doctor last night. As a result, I am going into hospital for a few days for observation. Nothing much, I'm sure. Just a bug I picked up on our last trip abroad, I expect. Pierre will scold me if he finds me still up, though.

He must never know about the money, of course, so do be very discreet, dear. He has very sensitive antennae, as you know. And can be fierce!

I was so happy, that last weekend we had together. How foolish of you to think my feelings could change, that we could ever be estranged! Whatever happens, bless you always.

Your loving
Claire.

"A pretty convincing case, don't you think?" he observed, putting the letter back in his pocket.

"You can't do this to him," she said slowly.

"I'm afraid I may have no option. But you make too much of it, surely. After all, it's past history now. We've both lost Claire."

"He has his memories. You'll poison them."

He shrugged his shoulders.

"You're too sentimental, Antonia. But nice," he added with a smile.

She studied his handsome face, utterly at a loss to understand him. Was he insensitive to other people's pain? Was he vindictive? An egoist concerned with nobody but himself? Or simply driven by a desperate financial situation? His self-possessed manner might have cloaked any or all of these possibilities. She thought of Pierre, learning that the wife he had loved so dearly had lied to him, deceived him, made a fool of him. She must have been a good actress. Pierre was too intelligent to be easily deceived. But then Claire was an actress; it was part of her equipment as an opera singer. A discovery like that would poison his life. He would live with it always.

After a long silence, he made a move.

"Well, I think I'll make my way to this fruit farm and see whether Pierre's at home."

"No, wait. Sit down a minute. If I could raise the money, would you give me the letter to burn and promise me never to reveal your relationship with Claire Valais?"

"Are you in a position to do that?"

"I've no money to speak of, but I do have a piece of jewellery my grandmother gave to me on my twenty-first birthday. It's old, and valuable, I think. I could sell it."

"What is it?"

"An emerald and diamond pendant, in an antique setting. It belonged to my grandmother's grandmother."

He looked at her curiously.

"You really do care for Pierre Valais, don't you? He seems to have a fatal charm. I hardly like to accept your offer."

"I seldom wear jewellery, in any case. It would only stay in a safe place. But can I rely on your promise? Are there any other letters?"

"I don't like your suspicion that I'm a blackmailer, Antonia. This money is owing to me from Claire's money, which is now Pierre's. And I need it, badly. That's all there is to it. So don't make unpleasant aspersions, or I might turn really nasty."

"All right. But it's all come as a shock to me, and I'm not used to handling situations like this. My money is as good as Pierre's, though, I assume."

"Well, I'm not saying that it wouldn't have given me more pleasure to have screwed it out of him, but on the other hand, it's by no means certain that he'd have coughed up, and I have to keep the main object in sight. Your certainty would be the best bet. That is, if it is a certainty. And, after all, since you're marrying Pierre, the money in a sense *will* be coming from him, so I need feel no pangs of conscience in taking it from you, after all."

"I guess your conscience leads a rather subdued life," said Antonia drily.

He smiled, his eyes creasing up in an attractive way.

"I like you, Antonia. A pity I shall be emigrating. We might have had fun together. That really would have been a joke, wouldn't it? To have shared both of Pierre's women. I'm almost tempted to stay, after all. If it weren't for those hounds of creditors, and the alluring prospect of making a pile with my friend in America. He has a flair for making money, which I, alas, so far have not discovered."

"You've got a nerve. When do you want this money? It'll take me a few days to raise it."

"I'll give you until next Friday. In cash please, my dear, not a cheque. And not here. I don't want to run into Paul Valais. I'll meet you outside the White Hart pub down the lane, at one o'clock. All right?"

"All right."

"And, Antonia, don't talk about this to anyone. And I mean anyone. Otherwise, I'll blow it sky high. That's a promise. I don't want any spokes put in my wheel at this stage. Understood?"

"Of course. You don't think I want to discuss it, do you? I'm the one who wants it buried."

"Quite so. But women's tongues are not always under their control. However, perhaps, like Claire, you know how to guard yours. Until next Friday?"

"Yes."

"If you don't turn up, or the money can't be raised, I shall go to Pierre the same day. Now I really must explore this splendid stately home. Thank you for your company, Antonia. You've been most helpful."

With a mocking little smile, he left her, and she watched him threading his way gracefully round the tables and out of the swing door, her eyes shocked and incredulous, wondering whether this past hour might not have been an unpleasant dream. It was not until long afterwards that she realised how cleverly he had played her that day.

12

An Ally

"You're quiet this evening, Tonie. Anything wrong?" asked Pierre as they walked along the river.

"No, nothing. I've got a bit of a headache. It was hot in that little shop today. More like July than October."

"Did you enjoy your party on Friday?"

"What? Oh yes. It was good to see them all again. And Nick came down to have a look at Willows' End on Saturday. It met with guarded approval, and that's saying a lot, since Nick is such an urban soul. Said it had atmosphere. I do hope the surveyor doesn't find anything terribly wrong with it."

"Nothing that can't be put right, I expect."

"And your meeting? How did that go?"

"Oh, pretty well. The architect has agreed to the modification we wanted."

"And the Directorship?"

"I refused, but they're leaving it open until the end of the month, in the hope that I'll think again about it. Don't know why they can't accept that I know my own mind. Once Joan Midway gets an idea in her head, it needs dynamite to shift it."

"She knows you'd be so good at the job. You're quite sure you don't want it?"

"I've told you. I have other plans. Forget it. How about

asking for a day off tomorrow, and driving to the coast? I'm sure Paul can spare you for a day. The season's coming to an end, and you never have any time off."

"I'd love to, but I've already asked for the afternoon off to go up to London to do some shopping."

"London? But you hate London, and never go there."

"I know. But there are one or two things I want that I can't get locally. And I'm collecting a copy of Nick's latest book. He's saved one for me. The biography of Cowper. It's had a good reception," she added hurriedly, anxious to change the conversation to impersonal subjects.

"And you like poetry. Seems a long time since you revealed that after your stroll along the Poets' Walk."

"And you were surprised, I think. I had the impression that day that you'd written me off as an outdoor type, knowing more about horses than the arts."

"And you, I seem to remember, were very touchy about it. Well, well. We've learned better. I'll be interested to borrow the book from you when you've finished with it. Cowper is right up your street, I'd say. He loved the country, too. And the simple life. You were rather unhappy over Darrel Brynton then, weren't you?"

"Among other things. A general sense of failure. I've forgotten all about that now."

"He didn't wake up past regrets?"

"How can you ask that, Pierre, when you know how happy you've made me?"

"I thought you seemed a little dimmed tonight."

She was glad that it was nearly dark now and he could not see her face. Still suffering from the eruption of Stuart Rockland into her life, she was hard put to it to mask her troubled thoughts. Never good at dissembling, she knew that she would have to make a tremendous effort to hide her disquiet from Pierre's shrewd eyes.

"I'm getting impatient with the job now that a much more inviting vista has opened up. For once, I found the customers at the shop a nuisance today. I wish the whole world would vanish, and you and I could be left all alone."

"And when I suggest getting away on our own, you tell me you have to go shopping!"

"I know. I'm very sorry. But I'm committed now. What about Saturday?" On Saturday, she thought, it will all be over. Rockland will have his money and disappear out of our lives.

"Sure. We'll start early and make a day of it. A walk on the downs, lunch at a pub, and then on to the coast for dinner at one of the hotels. Suit you?"

"Lovely. Look, you can see the reflection of the moon in the water down there."

"So you can. All wimbly wambly. Shouldn't you be quoting your favourite Wordsworth to me?

> Waters on a starry night
> Are beautiful and fair;"

She went on,

> "The sunshine is a glorious birth :
>   But yet I know, where'er I go,
>   That there hath passed away a glory from the earth."

"And that's a somewhat melancholy conclusion," said Pierre.

She turned to him as his arms came round her, and clung to him, needing in some undefined way assurance from him. She had a deep, uneasy sense that vague shadows were stealing up over the bright confidence of their happiness, making it tremble uncertainly as the reflection of the moon trembled in the disturbed surface of the river below them.

*   *   *

Realising her own ignorance of such transactions, she had

decided to turn to Nick for help as the only person she could trust not to probe. He knew the world and its ways. He would know where to sell the pendant, and was shock-proof. She had arranged to meet him at his Kensington flat that afternoon, and he welcomed her with his customary languid courtesy, looking calm and elegant in a well-cut slate-blue suit with a lilac pink shirt and a flowing magenta tie. She had never seen him less than elegant, and he carried his dandyism with a lazy air that was deceptive, for he missed little, and his mind was as alert as a squirrel's. At thirty, he seemed as comfortably settled in his bachelor life as a nut in its shell.

While Antonia prowled restlessly round the comfortable sitting-room which overlooked a pleasant square of grass and trees, Nick disappeared into the kitchen to make a pot of tea. Within a few minutes, he brought it in and placed it on the low table in the window. Inevitably, it was China tea with slices of lemon. He kept no other, so it was no use complaining.

"Now, what's the problem?" he asked as he poured the tea.

She had rehearsed it, but she blurted it out, her cheeks flushed.

"I have to find five hundred pounds to help someone out of financial difficulty. The only way I can raise the money is to sell the pendant Grandma gave me on my twenty-first birthday. I don't know how to go about it. I wondered if you'd sell it for me. I expect here in London you know the right place to go to . . ."

Her voice trailed away. Nick had ceased to pour in mid-cup and was staring at her in amazement. Then his eyes narrowed and he said calmly, as he filled up her cup and passed it to her, "Tell me more."

"That's just the point, Nick. I can't tell you more. I promised secrecy. I know it's a nerve, asking you, but there was nobody else I could turn to."

"Does Pierre know about this?"

"No. And he mustn't."

"Well, I'm used to the family looking on me as a kind of universal uncle, though I can't think why. It's the last role I'd choose. But I'm blowed if I'll do this without knowing the reason why. Who is this someone? And why on earth should you sell a family heirloom to help him or her?"

"I can't tell you."

"Then it's no go. Try a slice of lemon in your tea."

She looked at him helplessly. She had not anticipated this reaction, but knew him well enough to know that he would not be budged.

"Then give me the name of a reputable jeweller where I can take it."

"No. You'd need to have it valued first by a disinterested party, anyway."

"I can't tell you any more, Nick."

"If it were anyone else, I'd say you were being blackmailed. But since you're such a blameless character, my dear, I guess somebody is taking advantage of your generous nature and your gullibility."

"I'll have to tackle it on my own, then."

"If you do, I shall blow the gaffe to Grandma and any other Rainwood within earshot."

"You wouldn't, Nick!"

"I would. I'll not stand by and let someone rob an innocent like you. Hadn't you better tell me about it?" he added gently, seeing her distress.

"Will you give me your word that you won't repeat it to a single soul, ever?"

"All right. If that's the condition, I give you my word."

And then she told him of her meeting with Stuart Rockland. He listened without interruption, his face thoughtful. When she had finished, he said, "That letter. Was it quite conclusive?"

"Yes."

"Aren't you taking it too seriously? After all, it's past history. Pierre is involved with you now. It's the present and future with you that matter most now. Would it be so damaging, that discovery about his first wife?"

"Wouldn't it be to you, if you'd loved her so deeply and believed she loved you in the same way? That marriage was an exceptional one. I've heard it from several sources. From Pierre's grandmother, from people in the musical world who knew them well. A true marriage of minds and hearts, they said. I know that Pierre loved her as I'm sure he'll never love another woman. If he found out the truth, it would embitter and sour the rest of his life."

"You're a romantic, Tonie. I can appreciate all that, but I can't help thinking that however bitter the taste of past betrayal, the knowledge that he's now engaged to the most transparently honest person anyone could possibly find must help him to erase the past."

"That might be the case with some people, but Pierre is a man of intense feelings. The past is still very much alive for him. Claire's death was a devastating blow. I've helped him there. But, believe me, this revelation would be terribly damaging, and there's no reason why he should ever know of it now."

"But he's a man of the world, Tonie. Experienced. You're an idealist. At this distance, he could probably accept that his wife had been swept away on what might have been an ephemeral attraction for this character."

"With the lies that must have gone with it?" demanded Antonia fiercely. "I'd never be able to forget. Not if I'd put as much into it as Pierre had."

"No, I think perhaps you wouldn't. I've told you before. Too much intensity, too little compromise. But compromise, my dear girl, is very necessary, the world being what it is."

"Then will you help me now, Nick?"

"So you'll sell part of the family heritage? Grandma would not be pleased."

"I know. I only hope she never asks me why I don't wear the pendant on festive occasions."

"Let's have a look at it."

She gave him the case and he drew out the pendant and held it up so that the emerald glowed and the diamonds surrounding it flashed in the sunlight.

"It's a pretty piece. Worth a good deal more than five hundred, I'd say. Eugénie must have looked impressive, loaded with the pieces Grandma's been bestowing on her grand-daughters in recent years. This did belong to Eugénie, I take it?"

"Grandma's grandmother, I was told."

"Yes, that's Eugénie. A good-looker, like Grandma. Terribly patrician. One wouldn't take any liberties with her, if the photograph I saw in the family album is anything to go by. But then, of course, you never can tell what's underneath. You know, I don't feel inclined to let this go out of the family in this foolish way, Tonie. In time of need, perhaps. But not to bail out a two-faced twister like Rockland."

"I seldom wear jewellery. It doesn't appeal to me much. I'm not the type to show it off properly, anyway. Pierre's peace of mind means much more to me."

"I tell you what I'll do. I'll keep the pendant, give you the five hundred pounds, and you can redeem it any time you want to."

"Can you, Nick? I don't feel I ought to let you foot the bill."

"I shall have the pendant, worth much more than five hundred. I dare say, when you're celebrating your silver wedding, you may consider Pierre mature enough to know the truth about his first wife, and he can then redeem it for you. Is it a deal?"

"Bless you, Nick. I'm so grateful. It will relieve my conscience over Grandma, and save the day for Pierre. Are you sure you can afford it?"

"I expect so. My books are taking on a new lease of life in America, which makes the outlook quite rosy. Think no more of it. Not that I'm altogether convinced that you're acting wisely, but knowing you, I guess I'd better save my breath. Perhaps Pierre will inject some worldly wisdom into you over the years. Another cup of tea?"

Smiling fondly at him, she accepted another cup of what she considered a noxious potion by way of expressing her gratitude.

"I knew I could rely on you, Nick."

"The family handyman. Good for godfatherly duties, although I can't bear children; called in as best man although I shudder at the thought of marriage; remembered as an extra solitary male at dinners where the sexes want balancing, although dinner-parties, except when I choose the guests, are not my favourite pastime. And to cap it all, although of a solitary nature, I'm a member of an enormous family whose tentacles reach out to me wherever I am, and all my female cousins seem to regard me as a father confessor, for which role nobody could be less suited," he concluded plaintively.

"It's that cool, sceptical air that does it. Because you're not involved with the various family factions, we can all turn to you for objective advice. The looker-on. You should have a medal for services rendered."

"Well, let's get back to practicalities. How do you want this money?"

"In cash, he said."

"He would. Well, I don't carry such sums around with me, and it's too late to go to the bank now. I'll get it tomorrow. Can you come up and fetch it before Friday? I've proofs on hand which need correcting and I'll be too busy to get down to you this week."

"I'll come up on Thursday. Be here about six thirty in the evening, if that will be convenient, and I promise I won't stop and hinder you any more."

"Right you are. I think I'll lodge this pendant with the bank. Break-ins are not unknown in these parts."

"Can I have the copy of your biography of Cowper?"

He had inscribed it for her, and she thanked him again, her eyes suddenly bright, overwhelmed by relief at having shared her problem, and touched by his kindness.

"I won't ever forget this, Nick."

"As long as you don't ask me to be godfather to your first child. I've run out of speeches," he said.

13

Cross-Currents

WHEN ANTONIA ARRIVED back from London on Thursday evening, she found a scribbled note from Pierre awaiting her.

> Looked in this evening and was told you'd gone to London again. What's the attraction? Will you have lunch with me tomorrow? Expect you at the farm about twelve thirty.
>
> >   Pierre.

He had called about an hour earlier, she was told. Tired after her dash up to London, faced with having to find an excuse for not lunching with him the next day as well as explaining the reason for her second visit to London, Antonia felt that life was uncomfortably complicated just then. Comforting herself with the reminder that in twenty-four hours' time, she would be rid of Stuart Rockland for good, she accepted the offer of a pot of tea from Mrs. Septimer, then walked through the estate to the lodge to telephone Pierre since there was no telephone in the cottage.

Mr. Septimer, looking like a wizened little gnome in his leather jerkin and trilby hat, accompanied her part of the way as he wanted to check the temperature in the greenhouses. He was a man of few words, but Antonia had established a quiet rapport with him, based on their common feeling for the natural world. His sympathy with wild life was balanced by a misanthropic attitude to the human race in general and the tourist hordes who visited Belmont Hall in particular. Mrs. Septimer, contrariwise, had little interest in nature but an expansive kindness for people which was reflected in her bright, good-natured face and the generous hospitality which drove her husband to seek refuge in the gardens he tended with such fierce devotion. With these two diverse personalities, Antonia had settled in most happily.

It was a clear, cold night with a crescent moon, sharp and clean-cut like a comma of steel.

"The first frost tonight, I reckon," said Mr. Septimer.

"Pity to lose the dahlias."

"Mid-October. Usually get the first frost about now."

They passed the silent, dark front of Belmont Hall, and crossed the lawn. There was no movement in the trees around them. No sound except the calling of an owl from the woodland. Mr. Septimer left her at the greenhouses and she walked on towards the lighted windows of the lodge, trying to work out what to say to Pierre. She could not possibly meet him for lunch since she had to hand over the money to Stuart Rockland at one o'clock at the White Hart. Not for the first time, she wished she had some skill in diplomacy.

On the telephone, Pierre's voice sounded guarded.

"Sorry I missed you. What took you to London again, so soon?"

"To fetch something I left at Nick's."

There was a pause. Then coolly, "I see."

"I rang to say I can't meet you for lunch tomorrow, Pierre. I'm so sorry. I'm having lunch with a friend who turned up unexpectedly last Monday to go over the Hall, and found me ensconced in the shop selling the guide. Not so much a friend. Just an acquaintance. But I agreed to this lunch suggestion." She wondered if her voice sounded as forced to him as it did to her.

There was another pause, then Pierre's cool voice again.

"Well, we seem to be unlucky. I called in this evening to let you know that I can't manage our day out on Saturday, after all. I had a call from David Penryn. They want me to be present at a meeting they've called for Saturday morning to discuss the opening ceremony and staff appointments. I shall have to go. Can we make it Sunday, or are you otherwise engaged?"

"No. That will be lovely. I shan't be going home this weekend. My family have some relatives staying and they want my room."

"Right. I'll look forward to seeing you, then, about ten o'clock on Sunday morning."

Antonia stood alone in the hall for a few moments after she had put back the receiver. She could feel that gap steadily opening between them. On Sunday, she must close it somehow.

Janet asked her to stay and have coffee with them, and she was glad of the distraction from her troubled thoughts. Janet and Paul seemed closer, more in harmony these days, she thought.

"I had a letter from Madame Valais today," said Janet, handing Antonia a cup of coffee. "Thanking me for the snapshots of Philippe. She sent you her kind regards and hoped you were learning to handle Pierre satisfactorily. What a sceptical old bird she is!"

"I rather take to her," said Antonia.

"She's never approved of me, but I do detect a slight softening of her attitude in this letter. Phil had written her a long, lively letter full of his school activities, and I think the old lady has decided that I'm not so bad a foster-parent as she thought."

"If she were here, she would know that she couldn't wish for a better home for him. He's gained enormously from it.

Lost all that tense reserve. Stopped living in a solitary, private world," said Antonia.

"You started the cure, my dear," said Paul. "A nice little lad. He'd been too long alone with old people. He's been good for us, too. Shaken us out of our absorption in our private worlds. Heaven knows what physical hazards he's going to inflict on us, though! Janet bruised her leg badly yesterday, playing football with him, and we're both committed to taking him to see Grandma Valais in January and teaching him to ski. It's years since I was on the ski slopes, and Janet's had no experience at all. We shall probably come back in plaster casts."

"It'll be fun," said Antonia, standing up to go.

"Could you wait just ten minutes and post a letter for me at the box outside the cottage?" asked Paul. "Then I'll be sure of it catching the early post tomorrow. It's rather urgent, and I should have written it earlier but was sidetracked by helping Phil with his maths this evening."

While Paul went to his office to write the letter, Janet tried to settle her stiff limbs more comfortably on the sofa and said, "You look tired, Tonie. Everything all right?"

"Oh yes. London air never suits me. All those exhaust fumes. Don't know how Nick can bear to live there."

"What about Willows' End? Has Pierre signed the contract yet?"

"We're still waiting for the surveyor's report." She hesitated, then went on, "Did you know Claire well, Janet?"

"Not intimately. She and Pierre were married a year before we were, and we didn't see much of either of them. They were so wrapped up in each other and in their work. And they travelled a good deal during the last year or two of Claire's life, when she was well known and appeared in several opera houses. Italy, Vienna, New York."

"She was beautiful, I believe."

"Yes. Dark hair, one of those lovely pale complexions, large dark brown eyes. Surprisingly modest, in spite of her great talent. Pierre gave her the confidence she needed. Why do you ask? You're not feeling threatened by a ghost, are you?"

"Pierre hardly ever mentions her, but I can't help feeling that I must seem a bit inadequate beside her."

"What nonsense!" said Janet in her downright way. "I hope you're not letting a legend give you an inferiority complex. Pierre's jolly lucky to be engaged to you, and knows it, I'm sure. It's all history now, Tonie. Past and finished with."

"Of course. Forget it. I'm so glad everything's worked out well here. You're happier now, I fancy."

"M'm. Paul and I had it all out. Both to blame, I guess. I've accepted the limitations to my career now. When you marry, you take on obligations you can't shelve. Any determined woman can sacrifice her own interests to her career, but few women can sacrifice other people's interests to it. Husband's. Children's. Until women can learn to be ruthless in that way, as men can, they'll always work with one hand tied behind their backs."

"But there are other rewards to compensate?"

"Yes, if you're lucky. And I am. I'm going on to part-time work at the hospital after this month. I need more time for Phil, and Paul can do with someone to fall back on when staff crises hit the functioning of the estate, once you've left. We shall miss you, Tonie. And don't think I haven't appreciated the way you've effaced yourself and steered Phil towards me during these past weeks. I should have felt a bit guilty about that if I hadn't known that Pierre has more than filled the gap."

Paul came back just then with his letter, and Antonia took her leave, turning at the gate to wave to them as they stood together in the lighted doorway.

The still, cold beauty of the night brooded over the lawns and trees and paths. The stars glittered frostily in the sky, the crescent moon now sailed high above the woodland,

and only the sound of her footsteps on the gravel path broke the silence.

Instead of walking straight back to the cottage, she turned aside across the main lawn, through the woodland strip out to the river boundary, and walked along the high bank until she came to the seat at the bend in the river. There she sat down, turning up her coat collar against the cold, remembering that hot day in August when she had sat here wishing that time would stand still, and Pierre had found her and asked her to marry him. Below her, the water glistened in the darkness as it flowed gently over its shallow stony bed. Even the old willow trees, so seldom still, were motionless and silent that night. The bend in the river, where they had decided to stop looking back at the past and instead to look ahead round the bend where tantalising glimpses through the trees promised so much. But the past could not be obliterated, and ever since that evening when she had met Pierre's friends, she had felt the past take hold of Pierre and carry him away from her. His attitude since then had changed; become cooler. He had seemed absorbed in that other world to which she had never belonged. A whole area in his life in which she felt an alien.

She remained hunched up on the seat for some time, until, chilled, she roused herself and stepped out briskly towards the cottage, trying to reason herself out of this mood of foreboding. She was tired after the hectic activities this week. The unsavoury business of Stuart Rockland had upset her. After tomorrow, she could put him out of her mind, and on Sunday she would bridge the gap between her and Pierre. She must. Too much was at stake.

*   *   *

Stuart Rockland was waiting outside the White Hart in a shabby grey car, and stepped out when he saw her approaching.

"Hullo, Antonia," he said smiling. "Glad to see you. Hop in. More private inside."

He held open the car door and she slid in. When he was back in the driving seat, she said, "I've got the money. Can I have that letter first?"

"You don't trust me?" he said, reproachfully.

"No."

"Well, that's frank. It *was* a debt, you know."

"I'm just making sure that you don't have it paid twice over."

He laughed and took the letter from his inside pocket.

"Only one sheet, then. The one I showed you. The other really isn't for anybody else's eyes."

"Both. I'll destroy the letter without reading the first page, once I know that it's the one you showed me."

"I've said before, and I say it again. I don't like your attitude. I'm not a blackmailer or a cheat. This money was owing to me, and now I need it too badly to pass it up."

"Very well. I accept that. But anybody cruel enough to blacken the memory of a wife in the eyes of a husband who cared so much for her isn't likely to have fine scruples."

"We're not all such ingenuous innocents as you, Antonia. Pierre Valais stole Claire from me. I don't feel conscious of any duty to protect his sensibilities. Rather the reverse."

It was the first touch of spite he had revealed. Up until then, he had played it so coolly that it was difficult to gauge the feelings beneath the urbane mask.

"Well, shall we stop analysing motives and treat this as the business transaction it is? I have the money you think is due to you. It should redeem the pledge. I'm only asking for a receipt, after all."

He laughed then, his urbanity restored.

"So you are. Here it is, then. I'd like to see you tear it up after you've made sure that it's the genuine document," he added mockingly.

She glanced at the first page, which was in the same

handwriting, read again the second page, and then tore both sheets up into small pieces which she stuffed in her pocket.

"I'll put them in the first litter bin. Here's the money. Do you want to count it?"

He glanced at the wad of ten-pound notes inside the envelope, and said, "No. I trust you, Antonia. I don't have such a suspicious mind as you. How about burying our slight differences, and allowing me to stand you a lunch in Kingsford?"

"Sorry. I have to get back. When are you off to America?"

"Next week. The first flight I can get, now that I have the wherewithal for the ticket. Thank you, my dear. You've paid a lot to protect the fine feelings of your future husband. I only hope he's worth it."

She slipped out of the car without another word and walked quickly back down the lane, dropping the pieces of notepaper in the litter bin at the entrance to Belmont Hall estate.

That's that, she thought, and resolutely put it out of her mind.

14

End of a Dream

ANTONIA WOKE ON Sunday morning to the steady rustle of rain. The sky was uniformly grey and it looked as though it held enough rain to last out the day.

Determined that nothing short of an earthquake would stop her from spending the day with Pierre, she set out in raincoat and Wellington boots and arrived at the farm at the appointed time. He seemed surprised to see her.

"Rather expected you to telephone from the lodge and put it off," he said.

"There's been too much putting off lately," she said cheerfully.

"True. Let's have some coffee and see if the prospects look brighter after that."

Try as she might that morning, the old easy companionship seemed to be absent. Pierre seemed edgy, forcing himself to make polite conversation.

"Doesn't look as though it's going to stop raining this side of Christmas," he observed, after they had finished their coffee.

There was a long pause, then Antonia said jerkily, "How did your meeting go yesterday?"

"Very well. And the lunch with your friend?"

"Oh, that was all right."

"Anyone I know?"

"Just a casual acquaintance. He's off to America next week, so I shan't see him again."

There was another pause, then he said purposefully, "Tonie, I must . . ."

He was interrupted by the telephone in the hall outside. When he came back, he said, "Excuse me for a few minutes, Tonie, will you? That was David. He wants some information I shall have to dig out from papers in my desk before I ring him back. Help yourself to books, or records."

He left her, and she wandered over to the shelves of records. He had an enormous stock, two shelves of which housed operas in their separate boxes. She took one down. It was *Otello*. Inside, on top of the four records, was the libretto with the cast. Desdemona, Claire Valais. At the back of the libretto was a page of photographs of the principal singers, with short details of their careers. Antonia studied the first photograph she had seen of Claire Valais. A beautiful, fine-boned face. Almost a wistful expression, with large dark eyes under finely arched brows. Impossible to see that as the face of a deceiver. A gentle, sensitive face. She read the details.

Claire Valais, one of the most talented sopranos in the world of opera today. She made her name in the role of Mimi in La Bohême at La Scala in . . .

She put the libretto back in the box and hastily replaced it on the shelf as she heard Pierre's footsteps. When he came in, she was looking at some sheet music on the piano. He hadn't been able to find what he wanted, and now delved into the drawer of a small bureau by the window. There he apparently found what he was after, for he went out to the telephone.

She continued to leaf through the music, unseeing, conscious of the past coming to life in this room. It was all about her. Claire's photograph in the libretto, Claire's voice

on the records, Pierre's involvement with the world of
music. She was irrelevant, she thought, in this room. As
out of place as a toy whistle in an orchestra. But this room
held the core of the man she was engaged to marry.

She put the music down and walked to the window,
watching the rain slanting down. With desolation in her
heart, she saw it clearly now. Understood how it had happened. Pierre, embittered by the loss of his wife, had found
in her some light relief from his bereavement, and had
mistakenly thought that she would help him put the past
behind him, make a new life. But the old life, after all,
meant too much to him for burial, and there was no role
for her to play in it. And she realised at that moment that
he had recognised this ever since the old links had been
re-forged by David Penryn and Joan Midway. And his
attitude to her had changed. She did not blame him. It was
quite understandable.

As she watched the leaves spinning down from the trees
on to the sodden grass below, she felt something die in her.
He had been trying that morning to nerve himself to tell
her. He was a kind man, and would hate hurting her. The
telephone had stopped him. She waited now for him to
break it to her.

When he returned, however, he seemed in a brisk mood.

"Let's equip ourselves for the weather and walk to Kingsford for lunch, Tonie. I could do with some fresh air."

"Me, too."

"Something I've got to talk to you about. You're looking
washed out. Sure you're all right?"

"Quite."

There were voices in the hall outside, and then Kevin
opened the door, saying, "Friend of yours, Pierre."

Joan Midway came in, a briefcase in her hand, as
though primed to address a meeting.

"I do apologise for breaking in on you, Pierre, but I
worked late last night on the prospectus, and thought you'd

like to see the first draft. Then I can make any amendments you may suggest and have a fairly definitive proposition to put before the meeting on Wednesday. As you said you couldn't be there, I thought I ought to get your opinion and advice beforehand. Otherwise, we'll never get the prospectus printed by the date we settled on."

"I told you I had complete confidence in you and David when it came to drawing up the prospectus. I gave him my ideas. But it's good of you to travel down here on a day like this. Let me get you a drink," said Pierre, affably enough.

"Thanks." She smiled thinly at Antonia. "Do hope I'm not disrupting any plans. I thought on a wet Sunday, interruptions wouldn't matter so much. The roads were mercifully quiet. I had a very quick journey."

Pierre went to fetch gin-and-tonic for Joan and sherry for himself and Antonia, although the latter had no real desire for it and was merely trying to appear sociable against all inclination at that moment in time. Joan ignored her, and spread out her papers on the table in the window.

After half an hour's study and discussion, Pierre moved an adjournment until after lunch, and drove them both to the hotel at Kingsford, where, over lunch, the conversation kept wandering back to the Claire Valais school, in spite of Pierre's efforts to bring up other topics which would include Antonia. But Joan, her dark eyes gleaming with enthusiasm, could talk of little else.

As though to tease them, the sun came out after lunch, and when it became obvious that the amendments to the prospectus were going to absorb more time, Antonia felt that she could be a redundant onlooker no longer.

"Do you mind if I leave you two to it?" she said lightly. "I think I'll go across to Eliot's stables and exercise a colt he's training."

"Do that, my dear. I'll join you later," said Pierre.

He walked down the drive with her. The air was sweet

and fresh after the rain, and raindrops on bushes and trees sparkled like diamonds in the sun.

"Sorry about this, Tonie. We seem fated not to get together lately. But the prospectus is important."

"I understand. Not to worry."

"How long will you be riding?"

"Oh, an hour or so. In the paddock, I expect."

"Well, if we're through in time, I'll walk across to the cottage via the stables, but it depends how we get on."

She walked back to the cottage, tense and unhappy, and changed into her riding clothes. At the stables she was given a friendly greeting by Ted Eliot, the owner, who saddled up the big raking chestnut colt for her.

"He's frisky. I wouldn't trust him with anybody else, but you're as good a rider as I've come across for many a day," he said, giving her a leg up.

"I'll gallop him along the ride for a bit first, so that he can let off steam, then give him some jumping in the paddock," she said, and patted the neck of Rollo, who responded with a toss of his head and an impatient sidling movement.

She let him have his head along the ride over the heath, glad of the wind in her face and the effort needed to hold him and keep balanced. Here, she thought, was one sphere where she could rule. And hard physical exertion, which called all her skill into play, was always her best remedy for a troubled mind.

In the paddock, she took him over the jumps. He was an eager jumper, inclined to rush his fences, and that day, in a reckless mood herself, she went at them fast, too, as though she had to beat the clock.

There was a slight look of anxiety in Ted Eliot's eyes as he watched her, and he did not take his eyes from her when Pierre came up and stood beside him.

"Not too fast," he muttered. "Don't tempt him."

"That's a powerful brute for a girl to handle, surely," said Pierre, frowning.

"Not this girl. But she's a bit daring today. He takes a lot of holding." He whistled and fell silent as Antonia put the colt at a high jump she had missed out before.

"This is madness," said Pierre sharply. No rider himself, he knew enough about it to recognise recklessness when he saw it.

"Bee . . . autiful!" said Ted Eliott, breathing out with relief as horse and rider landed safely. "But I think that's enough."

But Antonia had reined Rollo in and was trotting him back. The colt's flanks and neck were dark with sweat, but when Antonia dismounted and patted his neck and spoke admiringly to him, he butted her shoulder, evidently on the best of terms.

"He'll make a grand steeple-chaser, Ted," she said.

"Aye. He's a good one. You were taking them a shade fast today, I thought," he added mildly.

"He wanted to be stretched. No misunderstandings between us. I'll give him a rub down."

"Don't you bother. I'll see to him. He'll behave like a lamb for a little while now."

He led the colt away to the stables and Pierre turned a white and angry face to Antonia.

"What on earth were you showing off in that reckless fashion for?"

"I was not showing off," she flashed. "I didn't even know anyone was watching until the last few minutes. And I was not being reckless."

"That's a matter of opinion. Eliot was worried, anyway."

"I doubt it. He knows me. And he knows the horse. He's training him to be a jumper. I'm helping."

"To break your neck and the horse's."

The nervous tension of the day, only partially released

by the last hour's exertions, built up again and her temper flared.

"Allow me to know what I'm doing in this one respect, at least. I had that colt under perfect control, and didn't ask him to do anything he wasn't perfectly capable of doing. I might risk my own neck, but not my mount's."

"You were going too fast. What was the point?"

"Not too fast. I find a physical challenge good therapy when I have problems."

"What problems?"

"All sorts," she declared angrily.

"If you'd bring your mind to bear on them rationally instead of making these reckless gestures, you might do better."

"What do you mean by that?"

"What I say. Problems won't go away, you know, by refusing to face them and taking refuge in physical fool-hardiness. The only likely result of that is a broken neck."

His voice was savage and his eyes flashed with anger. She had never seen him really angry before, and remembered his grandmother's advice to meet it with passive resistance, but such an attitude was alien to her nature and she was blown like a kite before the gale of her own anger, although she dimly realised that it was not the riding episode that was the cause but a deep and unendurable pain inside her.

"I have never been thrown by a horse in my life. I wish you would confine your attention to your own world of music and leave me to judge in my own field. I'm not a child to be lectured."

"Then stop behaving like one."

"I was merely trying to salvage something from the day we were supposed to spend together. Since other things are so much more important to you, I feel you should hardly complain when I get out of your way and turn my attention to my own interests."

"I said I was sorry about the intrusion of Joan. I might point out that you were the one who was otherwise engaged during the week. And for rather odd reasons. A little honesty wouldn't come amiss."

And the injustice of this was like adding salt to an open wound.

"How dare you accuse me of being dishonest!"

She was almost beside herself with anger, and realising this, Pierre seemed to get an icy control of himself.

"I'll amend that. Less than frank, shall we say?"

"I'm not in the mood for lawyer's quibbles."

"You're not in the mood for any rational conversation at all. We'll adjourn until you're calmer. I've some work to do. Ring me some time next week, if you have an evening free," he concluded ironically.

"And I hate sarcasm."

He eyed her with cool deliberation, then said, "You need spanking. Go and put your head under the cold tap."

She watched him stride off towards the farm, her anger subsiding in a sea of misery. Then she made her way to the cottage, the day in ruins.

Unable to bear inactivity, she changed into a pair of slacks and a sweater and, on impulse, cycled over to Willows' End, arriving there as the sun was setting in a red glow behind a low bank of grey cloud. The overhung drive was dark, but when she emerged she was almost dazzled by the brilliant crimson of the creeper which swarmed over the front of the house, and had shed a few leaves, like drops of blood, on the gravel below. She walked round, peering through the windows at the empty rooms, then wandered through the two acres of overgrown garden down to the river and sat on a tree stump gazing at the willows, seeing only her broken dreams around her.

The quarrel had been foolish. Really only a mask for the serious breakdown underneath. And, looking back, she saw how the breakdown had been inevitable. How foolish she had been, rushing in with her usual enthusiasm, sure that a wonderful new life was opening up, peopling this house and garden with their children and pets, seeing Pierre working happily in one wing, herself working devotedly for them all. Moonshine. Like the Viennese evening. Why should Pierre find happiness and fulfilment with an immature ignoramus like her, after Claire? He had from the first only seen their marriage as a kind of consolation. Second-best. She remembered him saying that she injected sparkle into his life. Like soda water. But that was a thin substance to exist on.

The more she thought, the more she drifted down into a morass of self-denigration. Everybody had been surprised at their engagement. Surprised that Pierre had engaged himself to a girl like her. Jonathan. Janet. Joan Midway. All in their way had registered a sense of the incongruity of this match. She did not blame Pierre. He had never pretended that it was more to him than a consolation. Had thought it was the same for her. He could not be blamed because she had grown to love him so deeply. Because he was a kind man, he was finding it difficult to tell her that they had made a mistake. And she was finding it agonising and humiliating to wait for it. Better to maintain some dignity and help him out, perhaps.

Why should she feel so shocked and stunned? The pattern was as it always had been. The also-ran. Also-ran in her home life, in her jobs, with the two men she had loved. The fault must be in her, not in her stars. Character is destiny. She was just inadequate.

It was nearly dark when she walked back towards the house and lingered by the mossy urn in the paved area between the two wings. Odd, the empathy she had felt with this shabby old house and wilderness of a garden. From the first moment she had seen it, she had felt at home here. Had thought she was meant to restore it to what it should be in this peaceful setting by the river. She fingered the trailing ivy for a few moments, saying goodbye to another dream, then walked quickly round to the front, collected her bicycle and made her way back to the cottage, feeling so twisted and broken inside that she was hardly conscious of her surroundings, and narrowly missed being run down at a cross-road.

15

Flight

SHE SPENT THE next day in a state of agonised indecision. But decisions would have to be made. Her own job at Belmont Hall was drawing to an end. Pierre had soon to move out of the farm house. The contract for the purchase of Willows' End was awaiting signature after the surveyor's report due at the end of that week. And Pierre had only until the end of the month to decide on the Directorship of the Claire Valais school. The fact that he had mentioned none of these pressing matters lately only confirmed her belief that he was steeling himself to tell her that it was all off between them. And sooner than see their friendship deteriorate into a series of squalid rows, would it not be better to end it cleanly, without recriminations?

The last little lingering hope that she had of things coming right again for them vanished the next morning with a letter from Joan Midway.

My dear Antonia,

I do hope you will forgive what you might see as interference in your personal affairs, but my excuse is my long-standing friendship with Pierre and my concern for the future happiness of both of you.

I know Pierre wants to accept the post of Director of the school of music set up in memory of Claire, a project dear to the hearts of both of them. He is ideally suited in every way, and his gifts must not be wasted. He is hesitating because the life in London would not be to your liking, and your interests lie in other directions than music. Perhaps he has hidden all this from you, not wanting to ask any sacrifice of you, but, believe me, Pierre will not be happy cut off from the world of music he loves so much, although he needed this interval, perhaps, to recover from the loss of Claire.

As I'm sure his happiness means much to you, will you not make the sacrifice and urge him to accept the post? It will be to your own benefit, too, in the long run, for a frustrated husband is not likely to make you happy, either.

David and I both sense that Pierre is very unhappy just now. I think he may be at fault if he has concealed from you his own wishes in this matter because you cannot share his enthusiasm, but I'm sure you care for him enough to adapt to the life which suits his gifts and temperament so well.

Yours sincerely,
Joan Midway.

It was not a matter of adapting, she thought sadly, as she put the letter aside. It was a matter of an all-absorbing world for Pierre in which she could play no part, where she was irrelevant, as she had been ever since his friends from that world had reappeared. He knew that, and she knew it too.

And so she walked over to the farm that evening, determined to offer him his freedom, feeling like her own executioner. It was a mild, calm evening, and the air was full of the bitter-sweet smell of rotting leaves and moist earth. She walked slowly, almost dreading her arrival, and it was dark by the time she came to the farm house. It was in darkness except for Pierre's music room, where light

streamed out from the large uncurtained window. There
was no sign of Kevin.

As she approached the window, she heard music. She
could see Pierre sitting in the armchair, his profile towards
her, listening to a record. A woman's voice floated out
above the orchestra, pure and sweet. A melancholy song.
Vaguely familiar. She searched for the clue. Then she
remembered. Nick had been listening to a record pro-
gramme on the radio when she had arrived on her second
visit to his flat, and it was this music she had heard, for
Nick had waved her to a chair and enjoined silence until
it was ended. The 'Willow Song' sung by Desdemona
towards the end of the opera *Otello*, so Nick had informed
her. And this, she was sure, was Claire Valais singing
it.

The window was open at the top, and she sat on the
broad window-sill, huddled against the angle of the wall,
and listened to Desdemona's last haunting song before her
husband killed her. She wondered whether this was the first
time Pierre had felt able to listen to his wife's voice. Or
perhaps, if you were a musician, you could listen to a voice
with appreciation and not be hurt unbearably by the
presence of the voice of a woman you had loved and lost.
She did not know. She felt there was so much that she did
not know about Pierre now. Only that she loved him.

The aria came to an end, poignant and beautiful. Now
Otello's voice was mingling with Desdemona's. Antonia, her
eyes on Pierre, saw him lean forward, elbows on thighs, and
hold his head between his hands. He remained there, bowed,
as still as an image, and she knew that she could not intrude
on him then. He was immersed in his own world to which
she did not belong. Claire's world. She was an outsider.
Would always be an outsider.

Quietly, she stood up and walked away. When she
arrived back at the cottage, she went straight up to her
room and wrote him a letter.

Dear Pierre,

I am sorry about our row on Sunday. But it wasn't really about my riding, was it? I've felt ever since that first meeting with David Penryn and Joan Midway that you wanted to go back to your old world of music and accept the post of Director of the Claire Valais school. And that you have come to realise that the consolation pact we made is not, after all, a good enough foundation for marriage. And that it's not the life you want.

Your changed attitude over these past weeks and the enclosed letter which I received from Joan Midway, as well as your silence about any future plans for us, have made it plain that you regret our engagement. Please don't think I am blaming you. Because we were happy together for a short time, you were misled into thinking I could make you forget the past. But I couldn't, could I? And now you are miserable at the thought of having to tell me, and that made you less than kind on Sunday, and made me blow up, too. So rather than see our friendship end on a sour note, with both of us saying things we don't mean but which would be remembered afterwards, I came over this evening to tell you that I quite understand how you feel, and to release you from our engagement, but I saw you through the window, listening to *Otello*, and thought you would rather be left in that world to which you belong and I don't. So I didn't intrude, but am writing this letter instead.

I shan't ever forget the happy times we had in Switzerland, and since. For you, it was a bright interlude. For me, it came to mean more. I want you to know that I love you, Pierre. I shouldn't have agreed to marry you otherwise. It was never second-best as far as I was concerned. But you need feel no sense of guilt. You made it perfectly plain from the start where you stood. And I see now that it wouldn't have worked, because your real world is elsewhere, and is one I can't play a part in.

I'm packing up and moving on again. Shall tour around, and perhaps find a job to suit me somewhere. I shan't tell anybody about our broken engagement before I go. I leave that to you. I hope the school will be a success and that you will find happiness and satisfaction in it. Please spare a little time for Philippe. Although he is so happily settled now, he thinks a lot of you. And remember the happy times. I shall.

Tonie.

After that, she worked swiftly. Driven by a demon that would not let her pause, she told Paul and Janet that she was going on the holiday they had been urging her to take for some time, and which would bring her spell at Belmont Hall to an end. Then she paid Mrs. Septimer for her lodgings up to the end of the month, and said goodbye to them. After packing up the minimum of clothes in a rucksack, she stuffed the remainder into a large suitcase and drove off in a hired car from Belmont Hall just twenty-four hours after her abortive visit to the farm house, posting the letter to Pierre in the letter-box in the lane as they left.

She spent that night at her home, depositing her suitcase there, and left early the next morning before anybody was up, walking to the station and catching the first train to London.

She had spent little money while working at Belmont Hall, and reckoned she had enough to last her a few months. Beyond a quite arbitrary decision to get a train to Newcastle, she had little idea of where she would go, only a blind instinct to head for the solitudes of the Border country and Scotland, and tire herself out with physical effort to stun the devastating pain that was boring into her heart and mind.

16

Gone to Ground

JANET LOOKED AT Pierre's white, set face and could not
decide whether he was angry or distressed as she tried to
answer his questions.

"She merely said she was going off on a walking tour.
The holiday was due to her and we had both urged her to
take this last week of her employment here as a well-earned
holiday. She's been looking tired lately. Had no fixed plans,
it seemed. But surely she talked to you about it. Is anything
wrong between you two, Pierre?"

"No. I thought I was too tied up to take a week off
with her just now, and now find I'm not. I want to join
her, but find she's left no indication of where she's touring."

"In a bit of a huff because you couldn't go?"

"You could put it like that."

Angry, thought Janet, because Antonia had shown independence and gone off on her own when his lordship was
not available to accompany her. Just like a man.

"Well, you've missed the boat, I'm afraid. You'll have
to wait until she gets home. We shall miss her here. We've
grown so fond of her. She won't be far off, though, if you
buy Willows' End. I hope you do."

He refused to stay for coffee and strode off to the
Septimers' cottage to see if he could learn more there.
Sticking to the story he had decided on, he met with

sympathy from Mrs. Septimer, but no helpful information.

"There, what a pity! She'd have been so much happier if you'd gone with her. She didn't seem to be looking forward to it much. I expect she'll be sending you a card soon, though, and perhaps you can join her then."

At her home, her mother was even more vague.

"That's Tonie, I'm afraid. Off on the spur of the moment, saying nothing of her plans. We're used to it, Pierre. She's always been a roamer. I'm hoping you'll be able to put salt on her tail. Get her to settle down. Young people these days seem so rootless."

How little can you know your own daughter, thought Pierre savagely, and left for what he knew would be a very uncomfortable interview with Mirabel Rainwood. There was just a chance that she might know, or at least have some idea, where Antonia would be likely to go. But he wouldn't be able to deceive Mirabel with the vacuous explanation he had given others. She would have to accept it, though. He wasn't going to expose his and Antonia's private affairs to public eyes. But she was going to make him feel even more guilty than he felt now, because she had warned him.

In the event, facing Mirabel's dark blue eyes, he did not offer any concocted story. One simply didn't do that with Mirabel Rainwood.

"I can't explain, *Marraine*. It's complicated, and there's a lot I still don't understand myself, and which only Tonie can make clear. I've got to find her. And quickly."

"I'm sorry, my dear, but I have no idea where she might have gone. And if she's touring, I don't see how anybody can know. Tell me one thing. Is this just a holiday, or is she not returning to her home?"

"It's not a holiday. It's a flight. Why didn't she wait and tell me? Why rush off like this?" he said despairingly, running his hand through his hair and striding to the window as though the room was too small to contain him.

"Antonia has always been an impetuous girl, choosing to meet crises with action. You're worried, Pierre?"

"Yes. When she's unhappy, she's reckless. Physically reckless."

"What are you afraid of?"

"Oh, pushing herself in some way. Risking her neck. Accepting a challenge that could be too big for her. It's her way of easing the knots inside her."

"Knowing this, and with your much greater experience, Pierre, how could you let this come about?"

"Heaven knows! I've bungled somewhere, but Tonie's been hiding things from me. And we both seem to have misunderstood each other."

"Hiding things? But Antonia is the frankest person I know. Too frank, I often think."

"Don't ask me to explain, when I'm in the dark about so much myself. If only she hadn't taken this melodramatic way out! It's absurd. Disappearing, without leaving any word to anybody about where she's gone. Is there nobody who might have some idea?"

"You might try Nick. He's always been nearest to her in the family."

"Yes," said Pierre more calmly. "He was in Ireland with her, wasn't he? And she went up to his flat twice last week. Thanks, *Marraine*. I should have thought of that. Have you got his address?"

When Mirabel walked to the door with him to see him off, she said gently, "Don't worry too much, my dear. Antonia is a girl of some fortitude, and won't do anything foolish, I'm sure. Let me know when you find her, won't you?"

"Of course. And, *Marraine*, this is all in confidence. I don't want a lot of talk about it. We've come to grief, and at this moment, I don't know whether we shall come together again or not. Meanwhile, it's our own private affair."

GONE TO GROUND 165

"I understand. You'll need a good defence with Nick,
but he's discreet, as well as shrewd."

Driving off to a solitary and unwanted lunch at the
nearest pub, Pierre drew Antonia's letter out and read it
for the fourth time. He remembered her radiantly happy
face when they had discovered Willows' End. Saw her
putting that brute of a horse at that dangerously high jump.
Recalled her evasions of the previous week. And recognised
the grief behind the brave lines of the letter. Joan Midway's
note he had torn up after a furiously angry conversation
with the writer on the telephone that morning. Even now,
anger at Joan's interference and false assumptions was still
boiling inside him.

He wondered how he would fare with Nick. He only
recollected him as a fair, good-loking man, with a somewhat
affected manner and a cool wit. Making a name for himself
as a biographer. The only artistic member of the Rainwood
clan. And the only one likely to know about Antonia's love
affair with Darrel Brynton. He decided to tread warily.

When he telephoned, Nick said he would be at home only
between five and six thirty that evening, and Pierre arrived
promptly at five. He gave Nick the same explanation as
he had given Janet, to which Nick listened with drooping
eyelids and a sceptical expression.

"She said nothing to me about a holiday when I saw
her last week. Knowing Tonie, she might take off anywhere. Rather sudden, though, in the circumstances, wasn't
it? The pressure of approaching wedlock, perhaps?"

"Could be," said Pierre smoothly.

"Well, Tonie always was a back-to-nature girl when in
need of spiritual refreshment and all that. I expect she's
madly tramping through some wilderness, enthusing about
the simple life and the glories of nature as she goes. I'd
wait for her to get back if I were you. No civilised person
could possibly want to trudge along with a pack on their

back, and put up at dim little rural bed-and-breakfast places en route."

Pierre glanced at him sharply. Was he flying a kite? The face presented to him was as urbane as any politician's, but the shrewd eyes were watching him closely. He would have to open out a little more.

"It's not quite as simple as that."

"It never is."

"We had a misunderstanding. I'm very anxious to put it right. I hoped you might be able to put me on the trail."

"I see. Not so much a holiday. More of a retreat."

"Yes. I'd be more than grateful for any suggestions."

"Well, the only thing that comes to my mind is that she may be making for an adventure school in Scotland where a friend of hers works. She's been there before. They run courses for schools, and for business men in sedentary occupations who need working on in order to fend off their coronaries. You know the sort of place. Barbaric and primitive, I call it, but everyone to his taste. Sort of place she might choose to hive up in. Mortify the flesh, and all that."

"Can you give me the address?"

"Now you have me. Darrel Brynton would know. He's been there, too. But I believe the Bryntons are still away. Let me see. They went off to Madeira on the ninth of October for a couple of weeks, so they were due back yesterday. Like me to phone them for the address?"

"Thanks. They might even know if she intended going there in the near future."

"Doubt it. She said nothing about it at the little party we had just before they went off. In fact, she could only talk about you and Willows' End. Pity you couldn't be there. You'd like the Bryntons, I'm sure."

"Yes. Tonie's very attached to them, I know. And a certain holiday you all shared in Ireland rates as the high spot in her life."

Again Nick gave him that quick, sidelong look as he dialled the number.

"Eclipsed a little now, I fancy, by even brighter prospects. Such zest! Oh, hullo, Jean. Nick here."

Pierre walked across to the bookshelves and studied the contents while Nick held an affable conversation with Jean Brynton.

"Well, here it is," he said cheerfully, handing Pierre the piece of paper on which he had scribbled the address. "The nearest you can get by car or bus is Cairnoch, after that you walk across a mile of moor, get a boat across the loch and climb up a hill to the school. A survival course even before you've enrolled. Hardly the place to fight your way to unless you're sure the girl's there."

"Telephone?"

"Heavens, no! They probably rely on carrier pigeon. Looks to me as though you're snookered. By the time you find your way there, Tonie will be home again."

"Could be," said Pierre grimly. There was silence between them for a minute or two, then Pierre went on abruptly, "I think Tonie's been worried about something lately. She came up to see you twice last week. Did she give you any hint about what was bothering her? I've a feeling in my bones that there was something else, besides our little misunderstanding. That might not have arisen, anyway, if she hadn't been unusually elusive last week."

"I can't help you, I'm afraid. What about a drink? I'm going to fortify myself with a sherry before I get ready for a dinner I'm committed to tonight."

Pierre eyed the bottles Nick produced from the cabinet and opted for a brandy and soda. They were both fencing, he thought, and so far, this cool young man was getting the better of it.

"She did come here twice last week, I suppose?" he said bluntly.

"Yes. You don't think Tonie's a liar, do you?"

"I'm damned if I know what I think. She hates London, saw you only recently at the Bryntons', yet comes up to your flat twice in one week, ostensibly to collect a book which you could have posted or given to her at any of the family gatherings. In addition to which she made the vaguest excuse for not meeting me for lunch on Friday. No, of course I don't think Tonie's a liar. It's because she's so honest that she can't ever lie convincingly. But she was hiding something from me. I'm certain of that."

"You must ask her, then."

"I'm asking you, since you're here and she is not. I need to understand."

"I'm not at liberty to tell you. I promised silence. All I will say is that it was a little business matter which we settled quite satisfactorily, and which has absolutely no bearing on this ... misunderstanding," concluded Nick delicately.

Pierre stared at him in amazement.

"A business matter?"

"Precisely. And if you ever suspected that Tonie was not absolutely devoted to you, that anybody else got a look-in, I can tell you you're a blind ass and don't deserve her."

"I've come to that conclusion myself, but secrets don't help, even business ones," added Pierre sceptically.

"We all have a right to them."

"And I was given no time to put matters right."

"There I sympathise. Tonie is a most impetuous young person. Flinging herself in and out of situations with reckless abandon. You'll have to rationalise her."

"Well, I mustn't keep you any longer. I'll have to think out what to do next. Send a wire to this adventure school first, perhaps. You've no other ideas?"

"There are some Rainwood cousins up in Northumberland, and Tonie once had a job in those parts, and likes the Border country. You might try telephoning them. She *has* put you in a fix, hasn't she? Telephoning all over the place saying where's my girl? She's run out on me. I should feel a little annoyed myself."

"I'd be furious if I weren't so worried. But it's hard to be angry with Tonie for long. She always acts with the best of intentions," said Pierre with a bleak smile.

"Well, good hunting. By the way, does the name Stuart Rockland mean anything to you?" added Nick casually.

"Yes. He's my brother-in-law. Why do you ask?"

"Your *what*?"

"My brother-in-law."

"Oh no!" gasped Nick, sitting down in the armchair he had just quitted and putting his head between his hands. "Oh, that foolish, quixotic girl! Trust her to get it wrong. Born to be taken for a ride. I should have investigated it myself."

"And what does all that mean?"

"Ask her when you find her," said Nick weakly.

"What's Stuart been up to?" asked Pierre sharply.

"Not my secret. Just tell Tonie that he's your brother-in-law. She'll come clean. And that's the last time I lend an ear to any of my Rainwood relatives. They all use me as a father confessor, and land me in all sorts of trouble, when all I want is a quiet, detached life. Well, well. I hope this dinner's a good one. I need building up after that shock."

And Pierre, no nearer finding Antonia, and utterly baffled by Nick's statements, left in a state of confused anger and anxiety. All very well for Nick to take it so lightly, but he knew that Tonie would be desperately unhappy at this final failure after all that had gone before, and the thought of her eating her heart out in solitary places or seeking oblivion by climbing unclimbable mountains or riding some vicious horse, tormented him. It was his fault. Mirabel Rainwood was right. With all his experience, he had completely misread the situation. Meanwhile, his helplessness maddened him. She had been gone two days. She could be anywhere.

After a negative reply from the adventure school, Pierre

asked Mirabel Rainwood to sound out the Northumberland branch of the Rainwood clan, with the same negative result. He spent the remainder of that week in a state of pent up frustration, veering between anxiety over Antonia's physical recklessness, anger at her impulsive action, and occasional moments of illogical despair at the thought that it might be months before she chose to reveal her whereabouts to anybody. She might find work abroad again, as she had done after the debâcle with Darrel Brynton, and meanwhile attitudes would harden and he might never have the opportunity to mend matters between them. It was her way of meeting reverses. With no close ties of understanding with her family, when hurt she went to ground. It was foolish, but that was Antonia's way.

And then, just a week after her disappearance, when Pierre was getting desperate, Janet telephoned him as he was having his breakfast.

"It's Philippe's birthday today," she announced.

"Good grief, so it is! And I'd forgotten all about it."

"But Tonie didn't. He had a card and a book from her. The postmark was Cairnoch. Can't read the county. Know it?"

"Yes. Scottish Highlands. Bless you. I'll leave a present for Phil on my way there."

"But she may be on her way back now . . ."

God bless that boy, he thought, as he rang off without replying. He threw some clothes into a suitcase, and as a token of his gratitude, bought a football in Kingsford and left it with Janet, not stopping for more than a minute or two.

"I've a long way to go," he said briefly, and as he saw the questions lining up, he squeezed her shoulder and strode back to the car. She was still talking as he waved a hand and shot off.

*　　*　　*

It was nearly ten that night when he reached the little town of Cairnoch, and was relieved to find an inn that could accommodate him. After an early breakfast the next morning, he set out for the adventure school, following the directions of the inn-keeper. It was a damp, misty morning, and he took some pains to follow the track through the heather as directed, for it would be easy enough to get lost in the mist. The moor around him was singularly feature-less, and although he had a map with him, it would be of little avail in this poor visibility. The bitter-sweet smell of heather and peat was welcome after the previous day's incarceration in the car, and he strode out briskly. As he neared the loch, the mist cleared and a pale sun emerged.

A dinghy was drawn up on the stony beach of the loch, and an old man emerged from the nearby cottage as soon as Pierre arrived. He had doubtless spotted him some min-utes before. It must be an event to see a living person in this landscape. A man of few words, and those few in a Scottish accent which Pierre found difficult to understand, he rowed him across the loch and pointed out the school on a plateau half way up a hill. Pierre surveyed what had evidently once been a crofter's cottage, and had now been enlarged, and several outbuildings scattered around in a small colony. It all looked very austere, and he felt some sympathy with Nick's observations as he started to climb up the steep, stony path to the main building.

A pretty, dark-haired woman greeted him with a smile, and when he explained his errand, she said, "Oh yes. You wired us, I remember. I'm afraid I can't help you, though. We haven't seen or heard anything of Antonia. I'm Mrs. Magellan. My husband runs the school."

Pierre's misgivings leapt up again as he said, hiding his dismay, "I'm sorry to have troubled you. I had a card from her post-marked Cairnoch and made sure she would be here."

"I would have expected her to look us up if she was in

these parts. Peter, one of our assistants, is an old friend of hers. Would you like a word with him? It's just possible he might have heard. He's over there, working with my husband on the far hostel. The fair-haired boy."

But the tall, thin, mop-headed young man could not help either.

"Haven't heard from Tonie for months. Doubt whether she'd think of coming here as late as this, though. We've finished all the courses. Working on maintenance now, and extending the hostel."

After a few words with the owner, Pierre returned the way he had come. Nothing for it but to enquire at Cairnoch. In such a small place, a red-haired girl would have been noticed, and he knew enough about country life to be hopeful of picking up some clue. If he had stopped to think, he might have known that in this mood, she would avoid anybody she knew.

And it was the inn-keeper himself who provided the information, while Pierre had a late lunch of bread and cheese, and beer.

"Aye, there's a red-haired lassie staying with Mrs. McPhail at the cottage next to the post office. She was only meaning to stay a night or two and then move on, but she had a wee accident climbing, and she's biding her time there now. You'll be a friend of hers?"

"Yes."

"Well, it's wild country for a lassie to be exploring on her own, and at this time of year."

At the cottage, Mrs. McPhail, a spare, bright-eyed little woman with a voice which proclaimed that her origins were well south of the border, was only too happy to enlighten him further over a pot of coffee which she had just brewed and which she insisted on him sharing.

"Miss Mendyp went out this morning for a walk, taking her lunch with her, but I'm sure she shouldn't be testing out that leg yet awhile. She'll be back for tea, though."

"How did the accident happen?"

"She didn't say much. She was climbing. Her foot slipped on some loose scree, she said, and she fell some distance to a ledge. All bruised and bleeding, her leg was, and nasty grazes down one arm, too. I wanted her to see a doctor, but she refused. Laid up for a couple of days. She's still looking very pale and poorly. I'm sure I don't know how she got home in that state. I applied what first-aid I could. So white and exhausted, she looked. Really gave me a turn."

Once started, Mrs. McPhail was only too willing to talk about herself and Antonia. She was a widow, he learned, and led a solitary life enlivened by the odd summer holiday-maker, in whose affairs she evidently took a keen interest.

"Not that Miss Mendyp talks much. Only intended putting up here for a couple of nights. A nice young girl. A bit lost, somehow, I feel. She'll be better for seeing a friend," she added, eyeing him with some curiosity.

"Do you know which way she intended to walk today?" he asked, not inclined to embark on a heart-to-heart with Mrs. McPhail just then.

"Along the burn towards the loch, she said. No hills. Not with that leg. As a matter of fact, I expected her back. But she's stubborn about not giving in."

"I'll walk that way and see if I can meet her, then. I'm very much obliged, Mrs. McPhail. The coffee was most welcome."

"Not at all. I hope you'll come back to tea with the young lady. I bake all my own scones and cakes, and do a very good high tea."

"I should like to sample it," said Pierre with a smile, and made his escape.

At last, he thought, he was nearing his journey's end.

17

Coming in out of the Cold

ANTONIA HAD STOPPED for a rest on the bank of the stream where a boulder offered support for her back, and now felt too sore and tired to make a move although the sun had little warmth in it on that autumn day, and she felt chilly. She zipped up her windcheater and moved warily round the boulder to make the most of the sun.

The water flowed fast over its stony bed, and the sound had lulled her into a state of mindless inertia. Dimly, she was conscious of an aching leg and a sore arm, but in a detached sort of way, as though those limbs did not belong to her. She felt drained of life, and no longer wanted to think. She had exhausted thought in all those solitary hours of walking through a countryside which no longer seemed able to console her, to which she could no longer respond. She had lost the key to the old delights. And that was something that had never happened to her before. A deprivation she had not believed possible to add to the loss of everything else. It would come back, she thought. Some time. All that she had achieved was to exhaust herself physically and mentally. She leaned her head against the boulder and closed her eyes.

The sound of a jay screeching a warning made her open her eyes to see a man walking across the little humped stone bridge a short distance downstream from her. She blinked, then he waved and she recognised him, half wondering if she was dreaming. Painfully, she stumbled to her feet, then, forgetting her injuries, ran to meet him. She said nothing as he put his arms round her, being beyond speech.

"Well, *mignonne*," he said gently, "a fine old dance you've led me."

"How did you . . ."

"The post-mark on the parcel you sent Philippe. My dear girl, why on earth did you have to do it like this? Whatever the trouble between us, why run away without a word to me? Without giving me a chance to sort it out?"

She raised tired eyes to his.

"I couldn't bear it. I tried to tell you that night to save you having to tell me, but you were listening to Claire singing and . . . I couldn't break in."

He shook his head, looked at her gravely, then said, "Well, you're obviously exhausted and in no fit state to discuss anything. What's the damage? Mrs. McPhail told me you'd had an accident."

"Only bruises and cuts. I put the arm in a sling because it felt more comfortable."

They sat down by the boulder, and noticing her painful movements, he said briefly, "Show me."

She rolled up the sleeve of her sweater and showed him the arm, black and blue, and grazed from shoulder to wrist.

"It looks worse than it is," she said hurriedly, seeing his expression. "You know how easily my skin marks."

"And the leg?"

"It's bandaged."

"I'd like to see what kind of first-aid Mrs. McPhail applied."

"It's well strapped up," she said, rolling up the leg of her slacks to reveal bandages, which were slipping, and a blood-stained dressing. "Well, it was when I set out this morning," she added.

"And you walked all this way on that leg."

"I didn't feel it much," she said indifferently. "But I must confess I was reluctant to start back."

"I'm not surprised. You really are a careless little devil where your welfare's concerned, aren't you? Talk about mortifying the flesh! Is that your lunch?"

"Part of it. Mrs. McPhail packed far too much."

He eyed the thick packet of sandwiches and guessed that she had eaten hardly anything. He said nothing while he rebandaged the leg, and Antonia could read little from his expression.

"Well," he said briskly, when he had made a workman-like job of it, "we'll let the doctor have a look at you, because I think that jagged cut may need stitches, and then I suggest we have a quiet few days at a comfortable hotel I know near Inverness before I drive you home. You need a rest."

"Why did you come after me, Pierre?"

"We're engaged. Remember?" he said with such irony that she was rendered speechless. For the first time, she realised that beneath his solicitude, he was angry. But she was too exhausted to follow any train of thought, and plodded along beside him, accepting his arm over rough patches, using a stick he fashioned for her from some fallen wood from a coppice half way back, for her leg was aching and throbbing with the exertion of the morning.

*   *   *

With five stitches in her leg and a slightly better night's sleep than she had known for some time behind her, Antonia packed her rucksack the next morning and meekly waited for Pierre to collect her, still feeling too weak to question his authority and wondering when he would stop treating her like an invalid and tell her what was in his mind.

It was raining that morning, and the windscreen wiper clicked monotonously as they drove south. Nearing their destination, some of her old independent spirit seemed to revive.

"We've got to talk, Pierre, before I let you take me home. I'd decided to get a job somewhere up here. I don't want to go home. There's no place for me there."

"You're right. We've got a heck of a lot of talking to do, but I don't think you're fit enough just now."

"Nonsense. There's nothing wrong with my tongue. And do stop treating me as though I'm ill. A bruised leg and arm. That's all."

"You're as thin as a rake, and exhausted. You've obviously neglected yourself in a crazy fashion for the past ten days, and I feel that there will be a better chance of rational discussion when you've had time to rest and get some good food inside you."

"Knowing all the time that you're waiting to put a rational and civilised face on the ending of our engagement? I prefer my way. I gave you your freedom. You've no need to feel guilty. I don't like to have things drawn out. Go in for long rational explanations. I saw what the position was, and I acted on it. It's cruel to prolong it . . ." her voice trembled and she fought back the tears.

"You acted on it without consulting the other party at all. I don't like being ignored when important decisions are made, and I won't put up with it, either. And as I don't like arguing when I'm driving, I suggest we continue this conversation later."

She sat there, tense and unhappy, her initial and instinctive joy at seeing him now swamped by the certainty that he had tracked her down only because he had felt guilty, and anxious about her welfare, as though she was an unbalanced child liable to do something desperate. She knew that he had telephoned her grandmother the previous evening. Now he wanted to bring her safely home to her family, and explain kindly that they had made a mistake but, of course, would always be good friends. Her head was thumping, as it had done on and off ever since the accident, and her arm felt even more painful now than it had when it was first bruised.

The country hotel, set in its own park-like grounds, looked friendly and comfortable, but Antonia was too unhappy to be consoled by creature comforts, and said coldly, "I've no clothes suitable for hotel life. I needed to travel light and only brought slacks and sweaters."

"No matter. Anything goes nowadays. And in any case, I think a couple of days in bed would be advisable. That leg needs rest. And in my opinion, you're still suffering from shock after that accident, which I don't believe was as trivial as you make out."

She was silent. In fact, it had been a near thing. The shaly ledge which had pulled her up in her fall was fragile. If it had given beneath her weight, the sheer drop below would have meant serious injury, if not worse. And the scramble back with the injured leg had taken all her nerve and endurance.

Pierre had pulled up at the hotel entrance, but Antonia made no move to get out.

"It wasn't just a trivial tumble, was it?" he persisted, eyeing her pale, downcast face.

She shrugged her shoulders.

"It's past history now. And if you think I'm going to have a convalescent spell here so that you can deliver me to the bosom of my family in better shape, you must think again. We can have that rational discussion here and now, and then have a nice, civilised parting. I can look after myself, you know."

And then he gave her an odd little smile and said gently, "If you could see yourself now, my dear, even you wouldn't have the nerve to make that statement. We can't have that rational discussion now because we're neither of us in a rational frame of mind. I'm having to bottle up my anger at your crazy behaviour, which has forced me to drop everything and come haring up here after you, because I can't release it on someone who's as done up as you are. It would simply degenerate into a squalid row like the one we had over the horse-riding incident."

"But it was all in the letter. I told you I understood."

"Yes," he said explosively. "You *told* me. You asked me nothing. Just told me, and went. A damned silly, childish thing to do."

"Do you think it was easy?" she cried, gazing at him incredulously.

He drew a deep breath and took hold of himself then. Putting his hand on hers, he said quietly, "We've blundered, Tonie. Somehow, we've blundered and managed to smash up something that seemed good to both of us. Now we've got to search our hearts and minds and work out if we've got a future together or not. It isn't a simple matter. I realise now that our seemingly straightforward consolation pact didn't get down to the basics at all. I would like you to take a rest, stop worrying about it for a day or two, and then when you feel better, talk it all out with me, honestly and without anger. Will you do that for me?"

And she had no answer to that. She nodded, and opened the car door, but her leg had stiffened during the journey and Pierre had almost to lift her out.

After that, it was as though her over-taxed body gave up all resistance, and she spent the rest of that day and all the following day in bed, sleeping most of the time the sleep of exhaustion.

On the third day after their arrival, her natural resilience reasserted itself, and she went down to breakfast feeling ravenously hungry and ready to face anything.

"Stiff, but much better," she said in answer to Pierre's enquiry.

He put his paper aside, and observed,

"It's a pity your skin marks so badly. That bruise on your

forehead looks most sinister. If I get black looks, it'll be because I'm seen as a woman-basher. Painful?"

"No. Not now. As the colours get richer, the pain gets dimmer. It's not a bad morning. I think I might manage a short walk."

"Good. It's pleasant and easy walking through the grounds, and there's a summer-house to rest in on the boundary, with a splendid view across the loch."

It was a mild, calm morning, with thin sunshine breaking through the haze as they walked through the grounds towards the summer-house from which they looked over the low stone boundary wall across the loch, dark and still beneath them. The mountain peaks beyond looked stark and bare against the pale sky, but on the lower slopes near the loch, a group of lofty larch trees still trailed a few fingers of gold, and cinnamon-brown bracken added colour to the scene.

It was warm enough in the summer-house, facing the sun, and Antonia watched a hawk hovering over the far end of the loch while she waited for her own hawk to dive.

"That letter from Joan Midway," he said abruptly. "It was impertinent, untrue and quite uncalled for. I rang her up and told her so. Why did you let it influence you?"

"It only confirmed what I believed."

"Mistakenly, then. But why the silence? If that's what you believed, why, in heaven's name, didn't you say so?"

"You were . . . off-putting. You'd changed. Withdrawn into a world I didn't belong to. I knew, that Sunday morning when Joan Midway interrupted us, that you were trying to tell me that it had been a mistake, our engagement. That we'd really little in common. No, Pierre." She stopped him as he tried to interrupt. "It was true. I overheard Joan and David talking about our engagement that evening while they were waiting for you to move your car. Although I hated every word Joan said, and tried to refute it in my mind, I had to admit in the end that she was right."

"And what did she say?" asked Pierre grimly.

"That it was utterly incongruous for you to be marrying a girl years younger than you who couldn't share your world of music, and to settle down to a domestic life in the country, burying your talent. That after someone like Claire, I was a hopeless letdown. Joan thought you'd just yielded to a fleeting attraction and now felt compelled to go through with it."

"And you believed that?"

"Yes. Your attitude latterly confirmed it. I could only spoil your life, hamper your career."

"Well, what with Joan knowing what is best for me, and you knowing what is best for me, it's a pity neither of you felt inclined ever to go to the trouble of asking me what I thought. I told you that I had no intention of accepting that post of Director at the school of music, and that I had other plans."

"Because of me?"

"No. Because I'm more interested in reaching a wider and more adult musical public through radio, and in writing about composers, translating operas into English and being an independent freelance in any aspect of music that interests me, and they are inexhaustible. I'd worked that out for myself over the past years since Claire's death. I've no wish or intention of going back to any teaching or administrative post in any college or school of music. Is that clear enough for you?"

"Don't blow up. They were very old friends of yours. It was only natural that I should put some reliance on their opinions. They had known you so much longer than I had. And you seemed so involved with the school, which was, after all, a memorial to Claire."

"Joan Midway is a bossy, self-opinionated fanatic."

"And very attached to you," suggested Antonia drily. "But that's beside the point. If it wasn't because I was standing in your way, why did you behave so coolly, almost like a stranger that last week?"

"I was waiting for you to tell me what you were playing at, to find out why you were making excuses for not meeting me that wouldn't have deceived a child. You went, against my advice, to that party at Darrel Brynton's, and thereafter were completely changed from my happy, loving Tonie to a shifty, elusive and, I thought, worried girl. I knew you were too honest to deceive me for long, especially as you'd told me all about Darrel before."

"You thought I was involved with Darrel?" she said, amazed.

"Who else?"

"He happens to be married. Happily married. And I told you, I was quite over that."

"That was when you hadn't seen him for a long time. Before that party."

"It was confirmed when I saw him. Darrel and I will always be good friends. I love you. How could you think . . ."

"Well, what *were* you doing, running up and down to London? I thought Nick was your go-between, or convenient alibi. You were hiding something from me, Tonie. I want to know what it was."

"I can't tell you. But it has absolutely nothing to do with us now."

"Nick knows, although he wouldn't tell me. I went to him to see if I could find out anything. I couldn't, but he did suggest that I should tell you that Stuart Rockland is my brother-in-law. And what significance that has, I can't imagine."

She had turned to him, wide-eyed.

"Say that again. Stuart Rockland is your brother-in-law?"

"Yes."

"He can't be," she said, clutching her hair.

"I married Claire Rockland, his sister. What's he been up to?"

"Oh, the villain! Fool! How could I have been such a fool?"

"Well, don't pull your hair out. Just tell me what happened."

And she did.

"Good heavens!" exclaimed Pierre. "No wonder Nick reacted as he did. Five hundred pounds! But, my darling girl, *why* didn't you tell me?"

"How could I? Knowing how you felt about Claire. It would have embittered you for the rest of your life. And Pierre, that letter, the part of it I read, really didn't sound like a sister-to-brother letter. Really, it didn't. I'll tell you exactly what Claire wrote, as nearly as I can. I remember it accurately enough, because the lines kept going through my mind at the time."

He listened with bent head, frowning as she recited the contents of the letter, then said, "I see what you mean. Claire was very fond of Stuart, and he of her. She worried over him. He's completely amoral, as you've discovered, and feckless. But, in his way, he cared for Claire. And when it became apparent that she had a successful career in front of her, he sponged on her in the happy expectation of being able to do so for the rest of his life. There was no love lost between him and me, as you can imagine. He was jealous of me and I disliked him for the worry he caused Claire. Fortunately, Claire and I were abroad a lot, but he was soon on her tail again whenever we got back to England. I tried to stiffen her to resist his financial demands on her, but she was too soft-hearted."

"That weekend she mentioned."

"She'd been unwell. Needed a rest. I couldn't get away because I'd promised to adjudicate at a musical competition in the Midlands. Claire arranged to go to Southwold for a long weekend. It was where they had spent many childhood holidays. Stuart drove her there and they had a happy weekend. I knew nothing about the promised cheque, but she knew I wouldn't have approved. I'd heard too often about these wonderful business opportunities that presented themselves, only to fade out. And to think that the rogue was able to make a monkey out of you, too! And you sacrificed a family heirloom to keep the knowledge from me. Foolish, mistaken, still knowing what was best for me, and very generous and dear of you."

"Oh, the pendant didn't mean much to me. But I'm mad that I was taken in like that. He was clever. Not saying anything about his relationship to you until he saw how the land was lying, and then spotting so quickly how he could mislead me and use me."

"You're no match for the Stuart Rocklands of this world, Tonie. And your grandmother wouldn't be best pleased to hear your airy disregard for the Rainwood heirloom. We'll redeem that from Nick straight away. Good of him to save it."

"Yes. My favourite cousin. I've always been able to turn to him."

"And never to me. That must be my failure. In all of this, what sticks out a mile is that you couldn't talk to me. That you saw me across a gap. You could make sacrifices for me, decide what was best for me, but all as though I existed on another plane, detached. I think perhaps I've treated you too much as a child. Your grandmother warned me. Have I, Tonie?"

She hesitated, then said, "Yes. I think, at first, I cheered you up. We had fun together. But the serious side of your life, music, Claire, you never tried to share with me. What really mattered to you seemed to make me irrelevant. That's why I knew there was no future in it. Marriage can't succeed on that basis. Your real life, a thing apart, and me just for entertainment."

"And that hurt."

"Too much to be bearable."

"And so you tried to knock yourself insensible."

"Not quite as drastic as that. I thought I'd find comfort in the countryside on my own. I have before. This time, it didn't work. But don't think there's any blame attached to you, or me, either. It's easy to make that kind of mistake."

"Let me correct one thing. You were never just for entertainment. You made me enjoy life again, but I care for you, deeply, Tonie. I was scared out of my wits when I saw you take that jump on that horse. And I've been having nightmares this past week, picturing you risking your neck in the reckless way you have when you're up against it. You mean a lot to me. I'm to blame, though. Somehow, by keeping things shut up inside me, I've made you think that Claire still stands between us, haven't I?"

"Claire and her world."

"Yes. Well, let me try to be completely honest so that you get the picture right. I've told you that the particular aspect of music which Claire and I shared is finished for me. Was finished when she died. Whatever you decide about the future, I'm buying Willows' End and shall work there on the lines I've told you about. As for Claire, I've not talked about her because it is still painful. The waste of that marvellous talent, as well as my personal loss. I loved her, Tonie. What I feel for you is a different kind of love. There's more than one kind, you know. I care about your happiness, I love your brave, gay spirit, and I want you in my bed and in my daily life. Claire is the past, you are the future. The past must dim. Time will see to that. The future is what we make of it, you and I. Affection, kindness, loyalty, just caring. I think that's enough to build on. But if it's not enough for you, if you want that complete passionate commitment I knew with Claire, and which I think is now burnt out of me, and if the lack of it will make you feel what you call an also-ran, then I shall understand and it will be better for us to go our separate ways."

"Would it matter very much to you?"

He took her hand and turned it over in his, studying it. Then he said simply, "The sun would go in, and it would feel very cold."

"And I don't think I should ever get warm again," she said, and he lifted her hand and kissed it.

"Promise me one thing, *mignonne*," he said gently.

"Anything."

"Two things, then, since you're in a generous mood. Never, never to know what is best for me without discussing it, and never, never to act on your impulses without giving me a chance to influence them. You can't marry me and still retain that sort of independence, you know. Have some respect for my grey hairs. I've grown a fine crop this past week, I can tell you."

"I promise. I've been so used to being alone, always."

"Then come in out of the cold, and get used to sharing," he said, and, avoiding her bruised arm, he drew her close and kissed her.

Her eager response blotted out the world around them for several minutes, until Antonia, to her own amazement, found tears streaming down her face as she leaned her head against Pierre's shoulder.

"Why am I doing this when I feel so happy? I suppose it's just too much, from one extreme to another."

She dried her tears while he watched her gravely. Then she gave him a wobbly smile.

"Sorry to be so silly. I really have been in limbo this past ten days. It seemed a miracle — you and me — then when it faded, it was ... Well, you can have one failure too many."

"You expect too much of life, *mignonne*."

"No, I don't think so. I always feel life has so much to offer, but the failure is in me."

"Your grandmother is a very wise old lady. She said your sense of inadequacy had been brought about by your family, and warned me that you were vulnerable. I should have taken more heed. Your manner is so gay and confident, it's easy to be misled by it. And now, it's up to me to repair the damage. You see, I'd been so shut up in myself since Claire's death that I'd lost the faculty for sharing."

"I understand. To have had so much, and to have lost it. I know I'll never be able to make up . . ."

He stopped her fiercely.

"No, Tonie. You've got it wrong. I must make you understand this clearly, or you'll always see yourself as an also-ran. How can I put it? You see, when you've got over the first desperate grief and have accepted a loss, you're diminished by it. The country you lived in has shrunk to a mere arid foothold. Loss of that kind is impoverishment in every department of your life. Your mind and your heart contract somehow. That's how it was for me until I forced my mind into new channels of work, and you came on the scene with your fresh vitality, and green grass began to sprout in my desert again. I was wrong ever to refer to our relationship as a consolation pact. That was trite and superficial, and diminished its value so that you saw yourself as merely my entertainer and were vulnerable to the first suggestion from Joan Midway that the time for entertainment was over. Correct?"

"More or less."

"Instead of realising that it was a gateway to a new and expanding life together. You mustn't think, ever, that it's a poultice we are putting on the past. It's something entirely new and challenging, in its own right, and will be what we make of it. Do you believe that now?"

"Yes. I do."

"And would have done so before, if I'd opened my mind and heart to you more fully?"

She hesitated, not wishing to put the blame on him, then said, "I was too impatient. You would have realised sooner

or later that I was no longer a child, and would have talked
to me about what really mattered."

"And if that's not damning with kindness, I don't know
what is," he said, laughing and putting his arm round her
waist.

"Music, Pierre," she said tentatively. "That means so
much to you. You've taught before. Now you say you want
to reach a wider public through radio. Couldn't you start
with me? I know enough to realise how much it can enrich
one's life. You probably thought I wasn't interested, but I
am. I need a guide, though. And with an expert to
hand . . . "

She stopped, surprised at the moved expression on his
face, wondering at his silence.

In fact, Pierre was at that moment rendered speechless
by her diffidence, which sent an engulfing wave of guilt
over him. She had offered him so much, given herself so
generously, and he had withheld himself like a miser, giving
her only the shell of his life. No wonder she had felt it was
not enough.

"*Mignonne*," he said at last, with a tenderness she had
never seen in his eyes before, "my sins of omission are
legion. Forgive me for being so blind and self-centred. I
promise to reform."

"Well, we've both made mistakes, perhaps, but we'd have
sorted them out without much trouble, I dare say, if Stuart
Rockland hadn't confused the issue, and I don't see that
either of us can be blamed for that. Let's put it all behind
us, and look ahead now. The surveyor's report. You said
you were going to buy Willows' End, so I presume it
wasn't too bad."

"You're not the only one to have irrational enthusiasms.
I take to that crumbling ruin, too. In fact, the report
doesn't contain anything disastrous."

"Good. I didn't think you were so keen, as a matter of
fact."

"One of us had to keep a toe on the ground. There's a lot to be done there."

"But we've all our lives to restore it. I prefer it that way. It'll be more our own, somehow."

"You don't mean you're going to do it all yourself, do you? Plumbing, heating, roof-tiling; the lot."

"Don't tease. As much as we can ourselves. It will be fun. Pierre . . ."

"Yes?"

"As I don't want to live at home, and you have to turn out of the farm house this month, do you think . . ."

"We could move in as soon as the contracts are exchanged? I was thinking on those lines myself. The house is big enough to hold us and the builders and decorators. A quiet wedding soon, then?"

"Yes, please. Will it be terribly expensive? Making Willows' End habitable?"

"We'll manage."

"And the five hundred pounds I wasted on that man!"

"Never mind. We can get the fundamentals seen to, and do the rest bit by bit."

"We could be self-supporting for fruit and vegetables on that land, you know, as well as having a lovely garden. I discussed it all with Mr. Septimer when I took him over it one day."

"You see what I mean," he said, gently pulling her ear. "All sorts of interesting new fields opening up."

"Not," she said reflectively, "that I wouldn't be happy in a caravan, if you were with me. It's just that Willows' End felt right for us, somehow. I saw our lives there; children, dogs, and us. And Philippe. A citadel against the worst the world outside could do."

"And much more comfortable than a caravan. I don't know whether it's the old farming blood in me, or just advancing years, but I feel an urge to put my roots down into the good earth. I've had enough of the mobile life.

Claire and I were nomads, really. And always would have been, of necessity. The prospect of putting roots down at Willows' End with you is deeply satisfying. We'll make a good life there, my love. Never fear."

And as they walked back arm-in-arm to the hotel, they discussed their plans for the home they would make, turning their backs finally on the bruising memories of the past, building for the future.

THE NIGHT OF THE PARTY

IRIS BROMIGE

Lucy Nevis's elderly employer, self-made millionaire Cornelius Wicklow, charms but dominates all those he meets. Returning with him from business abroad to the Wicklow country home, Lucy finds that his family do not all find it easy to accept his rule, particularly his grandson, Marcus Wicklow. Marcus troubles Lucy by his open hostility, especially when he warns her of his grandfather's ruthlessness. Though Lucy feels Marcus to be a dangerously attractive man, she cannot resist their growing relationship — and this is strongly condemned by Cornelius.

Tormented by loyalty to her employer, Lucy is faced with a difficult choice. Matters came to a dramatic head on the night of Julia Wicklow's 21st party.

CORONET BOOKS

ROMANTIC FICTION FROM CORONET BOOKS

IRIS BROMIGE

☐	20752 3	The Night Of The Party	60p
☐	19876 1	The Enchanted Garden	50p
☐	02917 X	A House Without Love	50p
☐	19892 3	The Broken Bough	35p
☐	19675 0	The New Owner	40p
☐	15107 2	The Tangled Wood	20p
☐	15953 7	Alex And The Raynhams	25p
☐	16078 0	A Sheltering Tree	25p
☐	16077 2	Encounter at Alpenrose	25p
☐	17194 4	The Gay Intruder	30p
☐	18281 4	Rosevean	30p
☐	18612 7	Rough Weather	30p
☐	12947 6	An April Girl	30p
☐	02865 3	Challenge of Spring	30p
☐	18762 X	The Young Romantic	30p

ELIZABETH CADELL

☐	10876 2	The Fox From His Lair	50p
☐	19863 X	Deck With Flowers	60p

All these books are available at your local bookshop or newsagent, or can be ordered direct from the publisher. Just tick the titles you want and fill in the form below.

Prices and availability subject to change without notice.

CORONET BOOKS, P.O. Box 11, Falmouth, Cornwall.

Please send cheque or postal order, and allow the following for postage and packing:

U.K. — One book 19p plus 9p per copy for each additional book ordered, up to a maximum of 73p.

B.F.P.O. and EIRE — 19p for the first book plus 9p per copy for the next 6 books, thereafter 3p per book.

OTHER OVERSEAS CUSTOMERS — 20p for the first book and 10p per copy for each additional book.

Name...

Address ....

....